a sojourn in time

frances
richardson

© Frances Richardson 2017
Cover Photograph: © Frances Richardson
Published by: daisyblue publishing
Box 224, Midland DC, Western Australia, 6936

IBSN: 978-0-9874023-2-5

For my son

Part One

Soho Fields, England, 1562

.

The Barn

There are times when one sees the normal day moving through the hours: the sounds known and part of your being, the touch of the table, the chair, the view from the window, the smell of bread proving. That day was like any other, at least like any other since Mamm died.

Those days were different. She would be there beside me, churning the milk, preparing the days meals, and talking as I helped with the tasks. My mother was the family talker and wherever she was, there was talk. Since then, it was up to me to talk but Tad often just looked at me and I knew to stop, because my voice is hers and I could see it pained him.

Since Mamm, of course, there was more for me and Padarn to do. Tad knew it was hard but I tried to have everything just as she would have liked. The hob cleaned every day, the table scrubbed, bedding aired and I made sure there were flowers in the vase she loved. Padarn did some of the jobs I used to do. He became much better with the milking: always good, never complaining.

I am afraid when he grows he will not remember Mamm. I know he missed her teaching him his words. I had tried to talk to him the way she did but he would not let me place his hand on my mouth. He signed that he could read my lips but I had to make him watch me, and he lost patience because I did not tell the stories the way Mamm did. Tad did not have the time or the patience with him then.

And so the days moved to a pattern without Mamm. We broke only on the Sabbath as we always did, to go to into Guiclan to worship. I let Padarn light the candle for Mamm. We always sat near the window of his saint. My brother is named for Saint Padarn, who we hoped one day would give him his hearing. My father never said that he no longer believed Saints concern themselves with us, but I knew that is what he thought. It was something I saw in his eyes.

I like to think that the saints would help us if they could. Perhaps when they die, their magic to hear us goes too. So they do not hear our prayers. But I know they still would help if they could and that their goodness is still with us. Mamm always believed that one day Padarn would have his hearing. She said he was born to sing. It was a good thing to think about: Padarn singing.

And thinking was what I was doing, thinking of her while standing in front of the bureau when I realised that the day was not like other days. There was none of yesterday's bread left and I knew there was still some after new day meal. There was also no cheese left and I had brought a new one from below only a day since. I had noticed this before but had not seen. And I realised that, for days, I had had to call Padarn to attend his work and his books. Something had changed.

Through the window I could see Tad and our cousin Edwore in the near side grove. Padarn was not with them. Perhaps my father had sent him to find mushrooms. The geese were down by the brook, the chickens scratching around them. The afternoon sun would have soon disappeared over the hill. Padarn was nowhere to be seen, neither were the horses. Their saddles were on the trestle, so I thought he might be feeding them in the meadow, but as I passed the barn I could hear their snorting from inside. When I went through the hatch, there were the horses feeding but no Padarn. I patted our old mare and laughingly asked her where my brother was and suddenly there he was: at my side.

> *Where have you been?*

He waved his hands.

> *Since morning – have you done all your tasks?*

He nodded. I asked him what he was doing. He lifted his hands. I was becoming cross and asked if he had taken bread and cheese to Tad. I could see him wanting to say yes, but he was always honest and truthful and would not lie. He then held out his hand and took mine like he used when he was smaller and led me to the back of the barn.

The man was lying on a bed of hay behind the bales. I looked at Padarn and he signed that he was sleeping.

Who is he?
He did not know.
When did you find him?
Three days.
Three days, sleeping? Is he injured?
Sleeping - eating - sleeping.

I thought Padarn wrong. He must be injured or with the sickness but he did look as if he was just asleep. I felt his forehead and turned his hands. There seemed to be nothing other than he was sleeping. His breathing was measured and normal. Padarn pulled at my sleeve and signed that the man said he must sleep.

He said this?
Nods.
When you gave him food?
Needs to sleep. A secret.

So this was where my brother had been. Watching over a sleeping man: feeding him and bringing him water. The man must have been about twenty summers and his cape which lay by his side was of fine green brocade. His hat and gloves lay neatly on his cape. He still wore his belt but his sword lay near his hand, as did his boots. He certainly looked a fine young man. I had not seen, even in Guiclan, such a finely dressed one.

What shall we do?
I looked at my little brother. He just smiled and signed Tad?
I do not think we should tell Tad. A small secret yes? Would you like to just let him sleep?
Many nods.
When he wakens then, he can just go on his way. The Saints would like us to take care of a traveller. And we need not worry Tad.
Again he nodded.
We shall see tomorrow. But you must come in soon. Else Tad will begin to miss you.
I left him guarding over the sleeping man.

As I left them I saw my father leading his horse through the top trees and knew he would soon be home. I hastened to see to the evening. As I did though I wondered about the young traveller who needed to sleep so much and why he did not come with a carriage or horse. It was good that Padarn had been a Good Samaritan. It is what his Saint would have done.

That evening was like any other although as we ate I could tell my brother was thinking about the young man and his secret. I was also beginning to feel guilty because I had never before kept anything from my parents, but I was sure Tad would not mind us just giving help to a passing traveller. We had done this many times, but they had not slept for days in our barn before.

And so we ate, and I cleared the plates and pots while Tad lit the lamps and Padarn began working at his books. When all was done, I sat at my loom and continued the fine silk shawl I was making for the daughter of our neighbour. She was to be married after the next full moon, and was only three summers more than me but she had made a good marriage with the son of a leader in the Militia Assembly.

It was then that we heard the horses and Tad moved to the door with a lamp. Padarn held up two fingers and I nodded. Tad gave us a warning - a be careful sign - before opening the door, and I signed for my brother to change his book. We heard Tad greeting the visitors and relaxed a little as my father brought in the Deacon from St. Augustine's and Councillor Gaewing from Guiclan.

Gwynara, drink for our visitors.

I was quick to serve them, returning to my loom to pick up my work. Soon we were listening to the reason for their late visit was to warn us. Councillor Gaewing seemed excited as he told Tad about a visit from the Militia in Guiclan. They had been after a group of Huguenots who had fled west and were advising farms to be wary of travellers who may pass our way. I saw Padarn's face pale.

6

Padarn – we need more wood, I said quietly, leaving my loom. *Father would our visitors like some of my cheesebread I made this morning?*
A good thought Gwynara, Yes, I am sure they would, and please some more wine.

I saw Theodane Gaerwing's face light up. Knowing he was partial to our cheeses, I hoped my bread was as good as Mamm's.

I cut the bread and spooned some of Mamm's precious olivemix onto the platter and took it with the jug to the men at the table. Tad looked up and nodded at me and I knew he was pleased. The food immediately changed the conversation to memories of Mamm and how they both missed her and her singing.

Returning to my loom, I signed Padarn back to his books with head down and tried to concentrate on the pattern for Elyzolda's shawl. It was difficult though knowing that we had a man sleeping in our barn who the Militia may be hunting. I was glad that they had come in the early evening and would want to return to the village as soon as they had exhausted their subject of the latest purge and of course, the food and wine. I was concerned also about my brother who just might give himself away, so I had to be careful to listen to the men, watch my brother and not spoil the colours in the loom.

I had just thought about the young man who might at any time wake up and come wandering to the lights in the house when the men began to rise and thank Tad for the repast and to again entreat him to keep vigilance in this difficult time and to be on the lookout for dissenters. Tad expected me to offer some more cheesebread which I did, but thankfully our Deacon raised his hand and again thanked us for our hospitality.

As their horses faded into the night, Tad closed our door and sighed.

Well, my dear children – let us away to the barn to see if our young man is still sleeping.

I could see my brother smiling and I too was more than surprised.

Tad!

Yes, I know. I discovered him before young Padarn here. We must let him sleep because he knew where to come and that he would be safe here. He will need to sleep for a while yet, so we will continue to safeguard him and make sure he has all he needs. No-one will know, except us. Yes?

Both of us more than agreed and a weight lifted from me. If my father knew of the man and felt we should help, then all was well. So, we went off in the chill of the night to make sure the young man was sleeping well. I took a coverlet and small pillow. We found him where we had seen him earlier although now he was lying on his back and one could see the detail on his top shirt and jerkin. They were fine indeed. He looked as though he did not have any cares and was happy to sleep in a bed of hay.

Tad said he looked well and that perhaps we might have a chicken as meat for the next day if I could sacrifice one of the chickens.

Yes, I have six chicks coming along. Padarn will help won't you?

He was nodding agreement and smiling. Tad looked at him with that pained look I always saw when it became obvious that his son could not speak like most of us.

Well done. You are a kind and good boy. Thank you for looking after this young man Padarn.

It was good to hear my father praise Padarn because he found it difficult to talk to him and had little patience with his signing.

The next day Padarn helped me kill and prepare the chicken. I knew he did not like to do this but as it was to help the young man he was eager. He made sure all the feathers were kept clean and sorted them by length so that we could get a good price. I spent the morning making bread, broths with the offal and salting the meat for future use. For the evening I cut some of the meat for a stew with onions and turnip. It would be good and Tad would be pleased.

When evening came we all went to the barn with broth for the young man. Tad shook him very hard to make him wake telling him he must eat and that his daughter and son would help him while he kept watch. It was very difficult to keep him from falling asleep but we kept shaking him to keep his eyes open and eventually he had drunk the broth although I remember much seemed to land on the cover I had over his jerkin. When he had drunk some water I told Padarn to go and fetch Tad and to keep watch.

Tad came and held the young man's hand, who then opened his eyes.

> *Thank you Monsieur.*
> *I have sent messages. They will come soon. Sleep now.*
> *The young boy?*
> *Padarn.*
> *And your daughter?*
> *Gwynara.*
> *Thank you Gwynara.*
> *It is a pleasure Monsieur.*
> *Sleep now.*

And so we left him, covered and comfortable. At least as comfortable as when sleeping in hay can be.

When we were sat at our meal Tad told us what he knew of the young man. He had not met him before but knew that many like him were being arrested by Militias because they did not believe in our church.

> *They are followers of Calvin?*
> *No, mainly a German Professor Luther. They call themselves Huguenots. But yes, they do not follow the Catholic teaching and wish to worship in a different way.*

That is wrong?
The Romans and others consider it so.

Padarn was trying to read us and signed.

Why?
Why indeed my son. An Edict has been passed to say they can worship as they please but many disregard this and the persecution continues. Our young man has been hounded out of his property and his parents killed. Some use religion as an excuse for other designs.

Tad did not tell us anything more. It seemed that he knew more of the young man but we just continued our daily pastimes including looking after what I now thought of as the sleeping man. I observed more about him as we cared for him and watched the hair on his face grow longer. Padarn thought this humorous especially as I tried to make him look fresh when I washed his face and cut his beard hair. I asked Tad about the markings on his jerkin thinking they were his family signing but Tad said that it was the Huguenot's Cross. It seemed they had a different cross to ours. Tad said the cross we knew was for everyone: just an ordinary cross. Tad did not think effigies of our Lord should be on the cross.

Padarn wanted to know why he slept, as did I, so one evening when Tad was moving the young man's arms and legs to make sure they were still healthy, I asked.

Tad, is it a sickness that makes him sleep?
No, my dear. This young man is a little different to us. Not only does he have a slightly different belief in the Almighty, he also has a gift which makes him unlike us. He has to have long sleeps to remain in health. To renew himself.
Does he not sleep at nights?
Oh yes, when he has had his long sleep, he is like anyone else.
It is very strange Tad.

Yes, it is strange. There are not many like him. Those like him, however, do much good in the world I have heard. So, my dear, we must always help those who are good among us. Yes?
Yes, of course Tad.

I tried to explain this to Padarn although I am not sure he fully understood, but then neither did I, then. I had always had faith in what my father said so I accepted what he wanted to do and that it was right. So, we continued to care for the young man until one day Tad came in early from the grove.

I told Edwore I had had enough for today and sent him home. We caught two rabbits and I said he could have both. As it is Sabbath on the morrow, he will not be here until two days. Come Gwynara, we must make ready. We will have visitors tonight.

And they came near midnight. Tad was near the door with a lantern and one could hardly hear the horses, so slowly and quietly they came. There were two of them and Tad ushered them in after they secured the horses. I could see Padarn was excited to see the coach but I pulled him back to the table inviting them to the food and drink I had prepared.

They were shaking Tad's hands and thanking him but wanted to see the young man before taking any refreshment. Tad shook his head when we wanted to go with them, but the one who was of the same age as Tad, said to bring the young people with them.

And so we all departed to the barn where the young man still lay, as before, sleeping on his back, covered with one of our best coverlets. Tad signalled for me to take a position by the door to keep watch. I could see the eldest man bend down and feel the young man's forehead, take his arm, hold it and then lean over with his head to his chest. He bent down and moved the young man's feet.

He is well. Thank you Andane. Only he remains of his family as you know. We need to be gone directly. Your son and daughter have tended him?
Yes, it was Padarn who found him and conspired with his sister to look after him, not knowing I already had found him.
I see. The boy cannot hear? He does not speak?
No, my wife was teaching him and Gwynara does her best to continue teaching him with signs.

The man began speaking in another language to his friend and he gathered the young man's cape, boots and sword while the friend just lifted the young man over his shoulder.

We shall adjourn to take your kind repast.
He looked at Padarn and signed – Come.

When they were seated at our table with the young man gently laid on the floor, they told their names. The eldest was Edwyn Woodcroft and his friend, Diarmad Brún.

And the young sleeping man is, Rodard Moorehouse.
Please to eat something before your journey. I know you must away.

It was interesting seeing these strangers with the young man just sleeping away on our floor. I looked at Padarn and saw that he too was committing all to his memories, much as I was. When they had finished eating, Edwyn turned to me

Gwynara, would you show me your loom.

I was surprised that he would want to see my loom, but then everything about that night was new. I took him over to my corner.

I am making a shawl for our neighbour's daughter. She is soon to be wed.
It is fine work. You are nearly finished?

Yes, I hope to finish it almost directly.
Work on it like the wind and have it finished by the Sabbath
and take it to them.
Yes, but?
A coach will come for you the day after Sabbath. You must be
ready. You will not return here. Your father understands. You
must bring your loom. Trust me Gwynara. All will be well.

I wanted to ask so many questions, but what could I do? My life to change? To travel in a coach?

And then the most wonderful thing in my life happened. Monsieur Edwyn turned to little Padarn and placed his fingers on his lips to sign quiet and then he placed each hand over my brother's ears. I saw both their faces as my father held up the lamp and watched the amazement on Padarn's face as he realised he could hear. Again Monsieur Edwyn signed – quiet.

Padarn? You hear me?

Many nods. And such a smile as we had never seen. What joy!

Andane, he must come with me. Tonight. You will come with
me – you will soon be able to speak – even sing! Understand?

There was but little time for us to express our thanks. They were gone soon after I had gathered things for Padarn's journey. The coach and horses disappeared into the night, leaving my father and me quiet and full of the change our lives had just taken.

I was soon to begin my journey, to leave my own country, cross Le Canal de France and after many weeks to arrive in Soho Fields. It is where little Padarn, not so little now, and I live with Monsieur Edwyn and his family. He has lessons with Monsieur's friend and cannot stop talking from the new sun to its waning, although at first his voice was so strange. I even hear him trying to sing some of Mamm's old songs.

We await the arrival of my father who has travelled through many countries to be here. He did not have as good a leaving our country as we had and has spent much time evading the Militias.

The 'sleeping man,' our friend Rodard, comes to see us often. He has found many other Huguenots who also escaped France. I have been visiting with them. They all seem to be as Christian as any I have seen.

I work at my loom of course and Monsieur tells me he knows I will be able to sell my silks. I hope to be proficient in the English soon. There is much to learn. It is a different life.

Part Two - Acadia

Applethwaite, Cumbria, England: January 1776

Remembering Acadia

I am writing this at the beginning of a new year and am reminded that it is twenty years since we left Acadia. I say left but it was never a leaving. It was an escape. One wonders where my sister and I would be now had we not been so fortunate. I am looking out at this winter morning as I write. Yvette tells me there is a hint of snow in the air. Januarys in Acadia were nothing but snow. I love the green that is forever here. At first, I could not believe it.

Father Copperfield used to laugh at me when I eulogised over this west countryside and how I loved it. "Good", he would say. "Let us hope it remains so." He would laugh then because he has little faith in hope. Of course, he is right: always. And now, of course, he would not answer to this name, having abandoned what we three had: our Catholic faith. Now he is not only our saviour, but our faithful friend Rodard, and our family pay visits to the chapel where we have become good Protestants. I am sure God does not think this amiss.

My memory of Rodard when young was just as "The Father." He would always stop by to talk with my mother and help in any way he could for my father. He would stay a few days, bringing us news of the conflicts, and then say he was off to another settlement, disappearing into the woods. He said we were lucky the mountain protected us. My mother was always, I remember, anxious for his safety especially from moose. The Mi'kmaq we knew, were his friends, some even Christian. Friends they proved to be when the expulsions began to take place.

There was always war at the gate, the British at war with the Colonies who wanted their freedom: the French who should have been our protectors but who seemed only intent on the war with the British. Both Rodard and my father agreed that we just seemed pawns in their war. The Mi'kmaq did more to fight on our behalf than the French ever did. I know my father would not join the Militias and said he would never give allegiance to anyone, especially the British. I would listen but I did not understand much of this at the time. We seemed away from it all. Our small farm gave us all we needed. We produced cloth, which we were able to trade with our neighbours and the Wabanaki.

I can recall my mother (I can still her voice), repeating every day at the sundown meal, the prayer of thanks for Acadia. She never wavered in her fervent belief that we had arrived in the Promised Land and that The Lord watched over us. When Rodard visited she would plead with him to lead the prayer, but he would smile and say, "I like to hear you and your lovely voice Ysayne." She would blush, my father would laugh and Morgona would giggle.

Our life, from my perspective was good: I knew nothing else. I worked alongside my father and I know my mother taught Morgona all she knew of domestic things. She was the heart of the home and had learned how to make baskets from the Mi'kmaq. She was justly proud of this together with her skill at transforming skins from the caribou and moose into garments.

I loved it when I went with my father to trade with the Mi'kmaq or they came to us. There would be much food and noise and I was allowed to sleep under the stars with my friend Taniel. He had taught me to use a bow. He would laugh at my efforts and say I would never be good enough because I was the wrong colour. I remember wishing to turn my bow on him but I always felt good after because I was better at the bent stick game than any of them. I told my father that it was their game but I was better at it. I can see him now, turning on his horse. "Pride, Dunane?" But he was smiling. I think my father knew what to draw from the scriptures and some that was best left quiet. It was wisdom, I hope, I have in my inheritance. There is that hope again. I smile.

But the boy that I was knew of the unease my parents felt. That in Acadia, we had roots. Despite this, we had become part of something that was threatened. Some Acadians had already left their homes to travel far into New France. Our neighbours were worried and some sons had gone to fight alongside the Wabanaki. I remember my father looking at me just slightly raising his hand to keep me quiet. His eyes told me that joining such a group was not in my future and I knew this to be true.

The Wabanaki talked of more British soldiers coming further inland. They were worried and Rodard with my parents began to talk of what the future might hold for us as Catholics. I would listen as I whittled. I remember the British taking Halifax though I did not realise the significance. And, I remember Rodard coming with the news that Fort Beauséjour has been taken from the French. I realised at this time that Father Copperfield was often with us and that he and my father would disappear for a few days travelling to the Mi'kmaq for news. My mother would always reassure us that all was well, but Morgona would look at me with those eyes of hers and I could feel her fear of the unknown. I would try to make her concentrate on our work because we had much to do with father away.

Then came the news of the Expulsions. The British wanted to be rid of Acadian and Wabanaki opposition to their plans to settle Englanders. Acadia would be no more. We would be forced to leave our homes and taken to the American Colonies. Many thought that it could not happen. Some joined in destroying supplies and whatever they could belonging to the British. But the British were winning their battles with the French. They seemed to be everywhere and we heard reports of soldiers being seen further north.

My father said he would never take us to the Colonies. I would listen in the evening when Rodard came.

> I will not take my children to become servants in Virginia. We have nothing but this farm. Will they recompense? No!

Rodard knew very well that whatever happened Acadians were regarded as French and Catholic and Britain wanted Protestant Englanders in what they regarded as their land.

> You must be prepared Theodane. I am urging everyone to be vigilant: and prepared. Acadia is becoming an idea that

perhaps belongs to the past. Some of the Wabanaki have helped the French by killing for gain. This does not help.

And it did happen. The British took Louisbourg and my father began to think we should return to France. Rodard thought this sensible as there were ships now taking Acadians back to the country from which they had fled. And so we began to gather our most precious belongings and look to the day we would depart. But then Morgona began to sleep and a few days later the soldiers arrived.

I was turning her, when I heard the horses and noise. I looked down at two of them talking with my father. They had the Moorsmith family with them. I wanted to go down but saw my father do his hand thing – just slightly and knew he wanted me to stay. Some of the soldiers began to sit under shelter and I could hear my father raising his voice.

We cannot go now. We have a child who is ailing. We will follow in a day or two." The soldier laughed.

And then I saw them. Saw it all. He was there, in front, with about ten Mi'kmaq breaking through the trees into the far field. My father sinking to his knees. The musket smoke. My mother's scream as she ran towards the soldier. The man turning, swinging his bayonet. The arrow slicing through his throat.

When the soldiers heard the Mi'kmaq, they began to run. I could hear Rodard shouting at them as they came. The soldiers did not get far, the Mi'kmaq dancing around them on their horses. Then he was with my parents, saw me, and signed me to come down. My father had already left this world but I was there to see my mother and to pledge to her my protection always for my sister. I have never, of course, wavered from this, but I know at that moment I could not conceive of how this was to be done.

I sat beside my mother, holding her hand and watching Rodard quell the anger of the Mi'kmaq telling them there would be no scalpings. He subdued all the sound with his calm voice and the hand held high. Their weapons were taken, the soldiers thrown together in a heap, the

Moorsmiths who were naturally terrified, were ushered into our home to rest. Rodard turned to me

> Dunane, we will need shovels. Bring me the Holy Casket from my horse. We must then look to your sister.

As he spoke, I also knew what else I was to do. It was the first time, looking at him, that he was telling me what to do without words.

The Moorsmiths joined us as Rodard gave my mother the rites for passing. All was quiet now, the Mi'kmaq kneeling with us and Rodard's voice as clear as the sunlight. I remember thinking how was it possible he had such a beautiful white mantel to place around his neck. The brocade dazzled the eyes. I handed him the small bottle of oil and he placed the sign of the cross on both my parents' foreheads as he said the prayers. My mother smiled as she tasted the dry rusk and sipped the honey wine. She looked at him.

> Rodard, Morgona sleeps ...
> Yes Ysayne, I know. All will be well, he replied.

And then she was gone.

He put the soldiers to digging graves and before sunset, we gathered around these gaping earth wounds to say farewell to my parents. He made the soldiers stand with us to hear the prayers. It was our friends and neighbours, however, who gently filled my parents' graves. Dedam Moorsmith wanted to know why Rodard had anointed my father who had already passed. Rodard smiled, put his arm around Dedam's shoulders and said.

> Do you think God would mind? Theodane was the best of good men.

That evening I remember being forlorn, sitting around an outside fire with the Mi'kmaq and the Moorsmiths. Our repast was small. Rodard insisted we included the soldiers who were roped together on the fence. The Mi'kmaq sang numerous verses of Ah! Vous dirai-je, *maman*, mis-pronouncing many words which made us sadly smile. Dedam still voiced his thoughts on the British lying feet from us but Rodard was adamant. They would not be harmed and definitely not scalped.

We left early the next morning. I had spent my time making sure the pelisse contained our most precious possessions and clothes for the winter. Mother Moorsmith had helped Morgona into my old clothes folding her hair under my best cap. She looked so frail, but just like a boy. The Mi'kmaq had made a cradleboard for her. She was wrapped and tied gently to it between two of their horses. We were many now together with our cow, the fowls and all the horses.

The soldiers were freed and divested of their hats and jackets. Rodard spoke with them before we left. It was the first time I heard him speak English. Looking back Father Moorsmith thought we ought to have fired the house. Rodard said.

> It is a good house. Let us imagine a good Englander family happy there.

It was not long before we were joined by a group of Maliseet. They were hunting and joined us along the trail towards the great river. There was much exchanging of information on the British, the skirmishes taking place and the farmers being taken to ships in the Fundy. Also, the best way to the river and beyond.

My thoughts all the while were for Morgona and I know Rodard was concerned. He was constantly moving, making sure Mother Moorsmith was coping, as she was not a horse rider, looking to the Moorsmith boys, and of course, Morgona. But Augustine and Ginnesh were making sure she did not move and I admired the way they moved the horses in unison. She seemed safe.

We quickly established a routine for the day, the camp, and keeping watch at night. Even the youngest Moorsmith boy was given duties. Father Moorsmith was good company for Rodard in the evenings because they had spent time in the same part of Brittany. It was good to hear them talk and smile at their reminisces. My main concern was, of course, Morgona. I was keeping a record of the days: what she ate and making sure she was turned and moved. It was good to have Mother Moorsmith with us because she was able to make sure there were no abrasions.

The Maliseet men left us after a few days but not before scouting ahead and assuring us the way was clear ahead, at least for a while. They took with them our thanks, plus our dear cow and a couple of chickens. The Mi'kmaq thought it would take us ten sunsets to reach the great river. We all wondered whether the British might be further down the estuary than we had heard. I can remember thinking how I missed my father being included in the discussions and plans. Today, I think my mother would not have fared well in our leaving Acadia: it would have been a challenge to her faith.

It did indeed take us twelve sunsets to reach the Maissimeu Assi. I remember our first camp night on the river, the men catching fish for the evening meal and a couple going further east to scout for British soldiers. They returned far into the evening with news that there was a large encampment we would have to pass a half a day away. Rodard and the Mi'kmaq spent the night with their plans. I was on duty that night and suddenly towards the dawn, there was more Wabanaki bringing canoes. Rodard greeted them and there was much laughter and thanks.

It seemed in joining us to help navigate the river, they were paying respect to my father and each came to me placing their hands on my head and on their hearts. I know also that they came for Rodard who they knew would be leaving and who had great standing with them. I did not know that then, but they came too for Morgona whom they regarded as "destined for blessedness." They thought of her as holy.

Soon everyone wanted to be away on the river and was busy organising the canoes: who would be together, the weight, the weaponry. Rodard though insisted that the Moorsmiths washed and changed their clothes, washing everything they could, for there might be little chance to do this for a while. I was to do this too. He lifted

Morgona in his arms and with Mother Moorsmith; he carried her a little way off to do the same. She had had her sleeping now for twenty sunsets.

And so, feeling rather damp but clean, we took to the canoes. I know the Mi'kmaq thought it as strange that we were so concerned with clothes. Taniel had always made fun of my breeches and I countered that it was heathen to run naked. I am embarrassed now at this memory.

That first day in the canoes was a strange experience. The canoes were of different sizes so there was much to organise. I had never been on a vessel of any kind and those of us from the land I think must have felt the same. I know the boys were sick that first day. Rodard rowed at the back of our canoe with Morgona and me in front of him. Taniel's father was to the fore. We made good time and late in the day, we came ashore to rest, make a repast and planned the night passing of the British camp.

The British has lit fires near the shore. Their light fell well into the river's centre and beyond. There were no ships, so the soldiers were moving further inland. We were in single file along the opposite shore well below the reflections. I could not see how anyone looking out across the river, would not see us passing.

We must have sat silently well into the night and then nature came to our rescue. A small wind. It blew the reflections of the fires towards the other shore. We watched and timed. One by one, the Mi'kmaq at the front of the canoes struck out when darkness hid our shore completely. It must have been more than one clock passing that it took us to slip past into the dark beyond. I turned to look at Rodard before we moved and he just smiled.

Towards morning we pulled into a creek, ate, caught fish and slept, for most of our journey would be during the late hours, or in darkness. Moving down river like this there were times when we had to take to the land and carry our gear and canoes. Rodard I knew was concerned about the weather and the time it would take to reach the estuary, travel southward and eventually find a ship to take us onward. Where we would eventually find our destiny I only wondered at that time and was apprehensive about asking too many questions. Questions plagued me from morn to the sun setting. Morgona was constantly my first worry with my promise to my mother. I knew to sleep as we did was dangerous and we were in danger every moment of the day. It was an added worry because she was frail and we travelled inhospitable terrain. I prayed inwardly that she would waken soon.

Therefore, we travelled sometimes during the day, sometimes at night. With the knowledge of the scouts who joined us with news every few days, we were able to utilise the daytimes to plan our journey and rest. We became close and more companyable than when we had visited their settlements. The youngest came around me to learn my language and hear the stories. They laughed at my **Wabanaki** pronunciations and I laughed at theirs. The early evenings were a time around the fire that I felt some relief. Morgona was sleeping well and she at least was taking some gruel. Rodard said evening prayers before our resting. It was a time to salve bruises and tell stories.

One day we were arranging to carry the canoes, as there were rapids ahead, when those ahead told us to drop the luggage and canoes and come – quietly. We lay Morgona under a tree and moved ahead. We came upon the rapids but the scene was one I remember with joy and fascination. The opposite shore was crowded with bears. They had sensed the coming of the season and were watching and trying to catch the first fish of the season. The fish, of course, never knew of the danger and some were getting through.

A couple of Taniel's cousins waded out from the shore and were rewarded with a couple of the fish, but the bears' roaring brought them back and we moved on. Rodard was concerned that the days were moving fast and we had much travelling still to do

One evening the scouts returned but with more **Wabanaki** from the north who brought fresh meat and roots. The news was good in that we were nearing the estuary. There were some of the men who knew the tides we would have to use to reach the sea, so they had come to help. I could see this affected Rodard who expressed his gratitude. That evening was a warm union, which was completed when Rodard gave us all communion. Looking back this was not really about Christianity, or any religion. It was about the human spirit and how these small rituals bring about the joining of people who are so different.

And so we came to the estuary. It was also a leaving of some of the Mi'kmaq who had been with us since leaving our home. Taniel's father and his two cousins were among them and I was sorry to see them go. I gave my cap to him to give to my friend.

It was a time of waiting again. There were two ships anchored a way off shore which were sure to see canoes breaking out of the river. We were then faced with fighting the tides and choosing the best time when we would not be seen: which meant in the dark. This worried Rodard and I knew Father Moorsmith thought it too dangerous but the Mi'kmaq knew the river, knew the sea and Rodard placed us all in their hands.

Whilst it remains a memory time of holding one's breath, the journey out into the sea and turning southwards was nothing compared to Mogana waking when we were tossed by a wave and the ensuing panic from me and the calming response of Rodard that I remember most.

I was holding on the side and actually looked down to see if the restrains were holding her when she opened her eyes. I felt Rodard's hand on my back and signed for Morgona to lay still and quiet. The panic in her eyes lessened. I could hear Rodard telling her in my thoughts, that she was fine, not to worry, that we were on the sea, and that all would be well. To just lie and trust us. And she smiled. She had been sleeping thirty days.

We were able to arrive in the morning light far from the estuary and take rest on the shore. We took turns to watch for ships coming up from the south but that day we were lucky. What was most sad was watching Morgona having to learn of the death of our parents. Rodard was (what would I have done without him?), thoughtful and kind and he related the brave ways in which they died together. He told how their last thoughts were of her and that he and I would be near her always.

I have not spoken much of my sister because at that time, I had never thought of her much other than someone I had to protect from all life's ills. As sleepers, we were a constant worry to my parents. They had never talked of this but I knew they expected me to be her guardian. No one knew we slept, so there was little to guard until now. Morgona was always able to hold her own in our small disputes which usually ended in a low silence when she would say, "Oh, Dunane!" and we would laugh. She has my mother's voice and even now I can hear that "Oh, Dunane!" To the world, she seemed frail, but she could lift her skirts and almost outrun me. She was as able with the axe as I was, and our cow always preferred her milking to mine. She was even better at the bow than I was. She was my laughing pal in those far days and my treasured sister now.

I watched the sadness being taken into her being as we talked of our parents and told of the prayers at our small ceremony around their graves. She looked at us.

> And do you think those prayers went anywhere, Father Copperfield?

I looked at Rodard and saw him smile.

> I think they went into the hearts of all who heard them, my dear.

And she smiled. You would have admired her bravery.

Our next days were spent hugging the shore staying just out from the breakers, watching for ships, slipping past those that were anchored at night and seeking the cove we knew would take us to another landing. Sometimes we could see the Ile Saint-Jean. It was a long grey shadow on the horizon. Rodard seemed to know exactly where we needed to

29

go and the Mi'kmaq and he were constantly talking of reaching Annapolis where there were ships taking the Acadians.

It was four sunsets before we found the cove we needed with the difficulty of taking time to survive the breakers without any catastrophe. This we did. It must be said that without the expertise of the Mi'kmaq we would not have made it with the ease we did.

Rodard insisted that we rest, as we would be travelling over land without horses and carrying canoes. This would take us to another river which led to the Fundy. I remember this day as the first time I ever stood with, I will admit, some trepidation in the sea. The Mi'kmaq boys and men had great fun disappearing under the waves, much to the mirth of Morgona.

It was time to cleanse, sleep, eat and talk. The Mi'kmaq was planning to travel much further north and find new hunting grounds. They would never surrender to the British, or New France. Rodard was obviously saddened listening to them. I remember asking him if the British would win and take all of Acadia.

> It will be a land, I think, where the British and the French will never quite cure their distrust of one another. The Wabanaki nation will not fare well.

We had no horses now, so the walk was harder. Canoes were either carried overhead, or on an improvised trundle. The youngest Moorsmith boy always managed to find a back on which to hang. Morgona was carried using slings between two Mi'kmaq. She said it was travelling like a queen and they laughed.

Our scouts were out front and we made good time that first day. We were making camp and looking forward to preparing for the evening and rest when we were suddenly surrounded by Redcoats. We heard just one voice, a British one, saying, in French, that we need not worry about posting sentries as we were surrounded.

I will never forget our capture. Although British, this voice was from a British Captain so versed in French, he sounded almost friendly with his instructions to lower any weapons. That the Wabanaki would not be harmed and he hoped that there was someone who perhaps, spoke English amongst our band. It was then that Rodard spoke.

Is that you Redmond?
Good God – Copperfield! Yes, of course. It had to be you!
Muskets down men. There will be no firing tonight! Relax. I am acquainted with this – fellow!

And then he came. His uniform was something I had only seen in some of father's books but he did indeed look splendid.

I see you have lost the cassock.
This is a little more comfortable for travelling.
So, no losing the faith.
Definitely not.
Well you must settle. Those are Mi'kmaq, are they not, skulking at the back there? You have them under control? I mean they are not going to do anything outrageous if I turn my back?
They are probably amazed at your uniform and wondering how they could steal it. It would make a fine trophy.

The Captain roared with laughter.

Come Rodard. Settle your flock then come and join me at dinner.

And so it was. Captured by the British, but luck was on our side. They had our scouts who had not been injured or maligned at all. They seemed to have had a splendid time exchanging trinkets. Mother Moorsmith and Morgona soon had our repast prepared and we did indeed, settle. Father Moorsmith was not convinced that we would not be harmed but seemed, as the evening lengthened, to become less apprehensive.

Rodard returned with much to tell although we all wanted to know what the meal he had eaten with Captain Redmond was like. Our diet of fish and salted meat with little in the way of vegetables was obviously having an effect. He laughed and described the meal accurately saying he ate little, as it would "upset my longing for salted moose." There was much to laugh at when he tried to describe what *sorbet* was to the Mi'kmaq. I watched Morgona listening to Rodard and realised that sorbet was as foreign to us, as the Mi'kmaq.

We wanted to know how Captain Redmond knew our Father Copperfield and Rodard told us that they had met while at the College de Sorbonne in Paris. The Captain was actually nobility, at least in England. He was Lord Clarence Redmond.

Whilst we still were asking many questions, the Captain himself appeared and Rodard introduced the Moorsmiths, Morgona, me and the Mi'kmaq. There was much laughter as Rodard, acted as interpreter, slipping from language to language. As he left, the Captain stopped by Morgona.

> *There is much talk of your journey from travellers. Rodard, I would advise keeping her as a boy: give her a new name. These are not good times to be a young lady of note. Good night my dear.*

We were up at light ready to go. Given four horses, our next part of the journey would be easier on everyone. We had gathered for what Rodard called – a short mass – when the Captain arrived with a few British Soldiers. I was immediately alarmed but Rodard stepped forward with a morning greeting.

> *Rodard, I have some miscreants here who would like to join your service. Not Catholics – well one says he is – but they say they would like to hear you and receive communion. Is it possible for you to accept some other type of Christian to your service?*
> *They would be most welcome.*

What a strange service that was: the sun under the horizon giving a soft blue light; the soldiers kneeling with Mi'kmaq, the Captain standing to the side. Voices and responses growing as more and more soldiers came quietly to kneel with the others. Rodard did not sermonise. There was no need. As he finished Morgona rose and went to a soldier, held out her hand, helped him rise and took him down to where Rodard was waiting. Thinking of this brings tears still. Men like the one who now held her hand had killed our parents.

All who wanted received communion that morning and by the time the final prayers were said, the sun was warming our backs. When we at last began to move, we had made many friends who stood and held their hands high wishing us good luck.

What we thought would be hardship overland was made much easier by having horses, added provisions and a sense of friendship we had not been expecting. I think these encounters with the opposite, although they may be fleeting, often bring us much to ponder. The warmth always a treasure.

We came again to a river but this was a friendlier one than the great Maissimeu Assi. Here, we said farewell to Gehue and Augustine's fathers who took the horses to return to their home. There was much laughter when they said they would take them back to the British.

There were a few rapids but these we negotiated. I remember it being quiet with trees sweeping down to the water giving shelter and privacy. We could see some settlements but passed them by without incident at night. Once we could hear music played by what I now know to be the Scottish bagpipes.

It took us just a day and two nights to come into the Fundy. The Mi'kmaq called it Chignecto. It was a sudden change to sea-born wind and a wide expanse of water. I remember feeling suddenly frightened by the cold wind, the dark water and the knowledge that we had reached the place where our fortunes would change once more for we could see the lights from ships at Annapolis.

Our canoes pulled in to the shore opposite. We rested and made final plans. The Mi'kmaq, the Moorsmiths and us knew this was goodbye. Only two canoes would take us across and we would have to make sure that our Mi'kmaq was not seen. We would need to be across before dawn and remain unseen.

Our canoe was to be first as we had less weight and could take more luggage. Our friend Gehue would row and the rest of the canoe would be covered with rush sheets. Rodard, Morgona and I would be lying almost flat. The Moorsmiths, of course would follow in the second canoe.

We sat ready watching the lights, hearing sounds brought across with the wind and wishing all would go according to plan. Rodard was explaining the layout of Brigs and that it would be good if we could come round the back of the last ship, as we were unlikely to be seen. Watching our friends, I am still amazed at how people listen so willingly to him and trust him to know and do the best no matter what presents. The Mi'kmaq knew exactly what he wanted and those watching their interaction knew the Mi'kmaq would use all their skills to deliver us safely on the other side.

Before our two canoes were ready, we had to say farewell to our good friends. I still remember this with tears. I had never seen any Mi'kmaq with tears but here they were. Rodard was visibly shaken, but Morgona held her tears and hugged everyone amid the bowing.

And so it began. The Fundy is an uncertain waterway with eddies and currents that only those who know water can negotiate. We were soon in the middle, Gehue quietly telling Rodard what was happening. We could hear sailors beginning to move on the ship. Then suddenly we felt the canoe touch a hard surface and felt Gehue slip over the side. He moved our canoe with him and then there was the softness of clay. Rodard was over the side before I knew and they brought the canoe about already lifting our baggages. Rodard signed to Morgona and she was away. I followed over the side and before I could think, we were on wet grass: Rodard clasping Gehue, Morgona kissing his hand, his hand on my head before he was in the water and away.

We waited amazed at how quiet and normal all seemed. We could still hear movement on the ships to the left. Rodard moved and then signed for Morgona to follow. We quietly moved our possessions up the small incline and took seat under a small tree. There was no sign of anything on the water.

Then a voice from the ship above us was loud and clear. "It's a bloody canoe, with Indians!" We too could see them. Augustine and his brothers, standing, waving their bows and yelling the best warrior cry I have ever heard. Their arrows began hitting the ship and sails. How Ginnish kept the canoe stable, I do not know.

When the first musket shot came, all four gave one final insult to the British and dived. The shots were aiming at the canoe. I looked at Rodard. He smiled shaking his head.

They will reach the other side without a breath.

We had to wait a while for the disturbed silence to quieten the ship's men. Soon there was a slight mist licking the water and from that mist came the second canoe. Yoshwa slipped over the side bringing it quietly underneath the ship. Rodard was in the water helping the boys, while the men helped Mother Moorsmith and the baggage. It was not a minute before we were saying farewell to Yoshwa and he was away into the mist.

As the sun-up began, Rodard was busy with the Moorsmiths. The eldest boy, Pierre was brushed down and a best coat was found for him. Mother Moorsmith also made good herself with a fine shawl. They were to go with Rodard. Father Moorsmith and I were to guard our possessions with our lives. Rodard, I remember turned to us as they left, he with Mother Moorsmith on his arm.

All will be well. Do not concern.

We could now see that the ship we had encamped near was *The Experiment* and I could see from Rodard's description that she was a brig. We could also hear that there was much activity now on the ship. We wondered and thought that perhaps one of these ships might be going back to France. None of us, of course, knew much about France, but it seemed the only place to fly to.

It was not one-half of the clock before we saw several sailors with Pierre to the fore descending to our encampment. The sailors began to gather up our bags and one of them lifted young André-Marie onto his shoulders. Pierre, feeling important, said.

> *It is triumphant. Father Copperfield says to come with the sailors.*

And so we went. Rodard was standing with a very important looking man, talking in English.

> *Ah, here are the rest of your Acadians. Come, we must be aboard for we sail immediately. Welcome all.*

Rodard looked at us:

> *I will explain all later.*

We hurried on board and were led below to where it seemed there were hundreds already. All were apparently Acadians. We found a place to sit and I can say now that we were all suddenly aware that we were seeing the effect of the expulsions. There was a pervading sense of hopelessness.

Within a short time, we could feel the ship move and people began to organise themselves. There were canvas sheets which we could hang to secure some privacy. As we were finding the best way to organise our small part of the area, a young mid-shipman, who must have been my age, came asking for the "Gentleman Copperfield." Apparently, the Captain had provided a room for us above. I remember Rodard looking quietly at us for agreement. The Moorsmiths I knew, as we all were tempted, but I saw Father Moorsmith shake his head, then Mother Moorsmith also. Morgona spoke for all of us as she said we would prefer to remain with Acadians. The young man looked a little shaken but thanked us and went on his way.

The next days were spent suffering the problems which abound in too small a space with too many people, minimum sustenance and little fresh air. I remember the smell to this day although the women were given time to gain the deck and perform such domestic tasks as they were able. Fortunately, the journey was short. *The Experiment* was a fast ship, the weather was to its advantage and we were told the town of New York was seen on the fifth day of sailing.

Many of the Acadians said they were bound further south, but Rodard insisted we all disembark at New York. He counselled everyone to leave *The Experiment* as soon as we docked. He had the Captain's word that there would be no sale of children on his ship. Rodard knew of the French quarter and suggested that they head there. There were however, near two hundred of us in the hold, and some were loath to venture abroad in an unknown town. The Moorsmiths I knew wanted to take their chance in the French quarter and find some way to earn a living. So much was unknown. Morgona and I looked to Rodard for our way forward as did many of the families he had talked to on the journey.

The Experiment docked and within minutes, we were jostling down the gangway into a new country. Rodard had organised a few fathers to be leaders and the families followed those. This kept us together and Morgona and I blindly followed Rodard who had the Moorsmiths and others under his watch. We walked through streets where many of us just wanted to stop and look but Rodard was walking fast and this meant little time to look. We had walked for about twenty minutes when he stopped at a house, ran up the steps banging loudly at the door.

A gentlewoman came to the door who immediately threw her arms around Rodard to the amazement of all watching. A few words and Rodard came back telling Morgona and myself to hurry up the steps where we would be taken care of. He then rushed down the line of waiting Acadians calling out the names of children who had been orphaned and looked after by other families on the boat. The children were hurried up the steps after us and we found ourselves in what none of us had ever experienced. A house straight from the books we had read but never thought of as real.

And then Rodard and the Acadians were gone. We were hurried into a sitting room where the gentlewoman told us to sit, yes sit. First, she wanted to know all our names telling us that she was Miss Elizabeth. Her French was interesting and I immediately detected that she might be English. But we all just knew by looking at her and hearing her kind voice that she was a friend.

It would be late that evening when we heard the door knocks and heard the very welcome voice of Rodard. We had a day which had seen us washed, given under garments and had our teeth scoured with wood and salt. Miss Elizabeth had had her servants comb our very matted hair and then proceed to cut the other boy's hairs and mine. There were eight of us and there had been a great discussion on clothes. Eventually we were all given new clothes. It was good to see Morgona in a skirt again.

The house seemed to have many floors and rooms everywhere and when we had eaten (I remember drinking a whole cup of milk), we were shown the rooms where we would be sleeping. Morgona and two other girls thought they were in heaven I am sure, because the room was all blue. The five boys and I also thought we were well provided for.

We were called for the evening meal as soon as Rodard came and were surprised to see even more children around the tables. All were quiet and waited for Miss Elizabeth to speak. She welcomed us – the newcomers – and told everyone our names. Some, she said, would be staying, some were only here for a while but all were safe, and I remember this, because, she said, The Lord was watching over us all. We then said Grace. As I heard the words, I opened my eyes and saw that Morgona, opposite, also had hers open. She smiled that smile which said, "Oh Dunane."

Before we retired that night, Rodard told us that we would remain with Miss Elizabeth until he found a ship which would take us to England. England! We had thought France was always our destination. This was not to be, he said. England was our best chance of a new life.

> It is a Protestant country, and we are Catholic!
> Morgona, we can be what we like. God will always understand good motives.
> The British thought their motives were good when they decided Acadians should leave their homes. Where was God then, Father? Acadia was my home. I was born there. So was Dunane and so were my parents.

I remember seeing the look Rodard had which I always had when knowing Morgona was right.

In the days following, Morgona was quiet. When we ate our last meal for the day, she would just listen to all the talk but not contribute. Rodard I knew was concerned but went out during the day with many errands for Miss Elizabeth and also to look for a ship that would take us to England. In the evenings, we would talk of news from Acadia, and those still arriving. It was always sad to hear of Acadia because it seemed that it would no longer exist and that we now had no past. We had become neither Acadian nor French, although that was our language. If we stayed here, we could become a member of what they now called, the New World.

During these days, we attended our first school for that was what Miss Elizabeth was. She was a teacher and had founded a school for orphans. There was a class for the girls and one for boys. And so, during the days - we would, as Miss Elizabeth said — begin to be educated. She was delighted to find out we both could read, Morgona much better than me. This helped, as we were able to say what interested us. Miss Elizabeth gave me many atlases when I said I was interested in maps and asked where New York was. Morgona just wanted to read, read, read and Miss Elizabeth said she all she needed to do with Morgona was to sit her in the library. She thought this the best education for Morgona.

Then one evening, after we had been with Miss Elizabeth for ten days, Rodard came bearing pelisses, which contained new clothes for us. We were to embark on a ship the next day to sail for Liverpool, in England. I know, even in the short time we had been with Miss Elizabeth, we had begun to feel anchored and safe. Rodard knew this and said we would soon have our own home. He promised.

And of course, he kept his promise. Within the turning of almost another passage of the moon, we saw the coast of England, landed at what I remember was the Salthouse Dock in Liverpool, and begun to make our way north into Cumbria. We had taken new names for the journey, Rodard had said, for safety. This ship's passage was so different to The Experiment. Morgona and I did feel as though we were different people, because on The Transient, we had our own cubicles. I suffered with sickness from the repeated turbulence but Morgona and Rodard spent much time with the sailors, helping with the ropes and sails. They thought her a strange young lady because she wore breeches.

And so we travelled through Cumbria to Applethwaite, which is where we settled with our own names, although Rodard seems to constantly become someone else. We spent some time in Keswick at The George until we found our new home here. I became a dayboy at the Free School boarding with the Master and his children. Morgona, of course, was jealous and I had to share all I had learned with her on my time at home. I thought her the lucky one because she had a Quaker tutor from the Quaker house in Keswick. As always, she was, and is still, much better at the learning than me.

Now, with Rodard, she teaches in a school for girls, which has more enrolments each year. Their free days are spent with Yvette, me, and our growing family. Applethwaite is far from Acadia and with the fall of Montreal, and the Treaty of Paris, a decade ago, the country where I was born no longer exists. Rodard says the Wabanaki will survive but not as we knew them. This is a sadness. Our small farm – a paradise – is far from them, Acadia, and its memories.

Part Three

London 1947 / Fremantle 1948

London, August 2nd 1947 – Bank Holiday Weekend

She had been dreaming of the battle. Her father always called it *The* Battle as if there had never been a battle before or since. But, as always, she now thought he was right. That had been a battle. It had only taken just more than a decade though to change things to where they had been in past times, with the windows boarded, the mobs out for blood.

Then, she had seen her father march and fight with the others, knowing that, for once they had fought back. With her mother, she had followed shouting: *We Are English!* When the mounted horses came, she had struggled away from her mother and joined boys throwing marbles under the horses. Then she had run at the horses' flanks with her fork. She remembered her father saying after - as they celebrated - that he was proud of his fighting daughter and that she must always fight the good fight.

Now, much later she had awakened to the roar of fire, to the knowledge that she could not move, that she seems to be covered in earth, to shouting somewhere far above her, to the over-whelming need to turn over and sleep. Stay awake. Fight it she thought. Where was her Mother? How long had she been asleep this time?

Sleeps never arrived when you wanted them. They had always planned, counting the years with always the mind's calendar saying: it will be this year. Now she lay forcing the sleep away to recall leaving her nursing post, arriving home to Stepney to find it once more beleaguered with days of violence and seeming hatred for anything Jewish. She had stopped at the corner knowing - hearing her father from the past saying – *round the back lovely one*.

****

Rachel had been there waiting, the door opening and closing without a sound, the arm around her shoulder guiding her to the basement stairs.

What a time you have chosen, my girl. No one saw you? Come, I have everything ready. Some of my best Sauerbraten? I have been saving the rationings. You will need it. Look at you. You work too long.

I have been fighting it Mama. I know now is not a good time: when will there be? Will it be too much? You must not lift me. Michael will help. Just tell him Mama. He knows what to do. He did grow up with Papa you know.

Enough. I will tell him tomorrow. Tsufridn!

The girl settled and asleep, Rachel moved into the shop, doing her nightly check, feeling her way between the tables. She lit no candle moving to the window thinking how she had been glad to see it again when the boards were removed during the street's end of war celebration. Now she wished she had kept them. Sometimes it is better not to look out on the world.

She could see the Morgans at their bedroom window opposite. They were straining to see down the street. Then she heard it. It was not a new sound. She had heard it in the outskirts of Krakow, on the docks in Southampton, in the years before the war. The sound of hatred. As it grew louder, Rachel rushed to make sure all doors were locked, kissing the door to the basement.

She turned, hearing the shop window crash and the whoops and cheers as she hurried back to the shop. They were still throwing bricks but then came the balls of lighted paper. She began stamping as they fell on the floor and as she turned thinking to bring buckets of water, she saw one fall on a bale of rayon igniting the curtains. She ran to the scullery scrabbling for the tap and bucket. People were running along the alley, gates were slamming and she heard Paddy's police whistle calling for help.

She over-filled the bucket and it splashed as she ran. The rush of heat hit her as she turned into the corridor. She faltered but ran on. The walls behind the counter were ablaze reaching for the ceiling. She saw it was also the gas lamps that were consumed. The bucket crashed to the floor as she ran back to the scullery, grabbing a chair and reaching for the gas stopcock.

The mob running from the scene stopped as they heard the explosion. Some of them cheered, others seemed anxious and then as one, they ran.

****

He was thinking there is something different in the smell of a fire in a building: very different to the smell of wood burning in the hearth. He was standing amongst the few gathered around the destruction of Samuel and Rachel Hellman's shop. They were watching the two policemen supervising workmen erecting a barrier around the still-smoking piles of timber, bricks, slate and glass. The hurricane lamps threw their shadows high against the remaining shops and houses.

He turned as another policeman joined the group, placing his bicycle against a lamppost. The policeman began talking to the remaining watchers, and then moved among them taking names in his small notebook. Gradually they moved away, their farewells held in the dark August night. Only the Morgans remained, seeming reluctant to take with them the events of the night.

The policeman walked over to the man who had moved to the far pavement. They shook hands, the man in uniform shaking his head. He then wrote in his notebook, removed the slip of paper and handed it to the man. They spoke a few words; clasped each other's hands and then the policeman joined his colleagues near the barrier.

At the end of the street a man turned the corner running, but when he saw the lights and the police, he stopped and began walking slowly.

The man on the pavement held up his hand. When they meet, they clasp each other's hands and hold their foreheads together. Their language is not English.

> This is England? Brother, this is England!
> I know.
> Richard?
> He is in Liverpool. It is bad there. Willhelm is with him. Gregor is in Manchester with Karl and his brother, Simon. Rachel?
> I was too late. There was an explosion. She was killed.
> I am so sorry Edwyn. The girl?
> She apparently left her nursing post yesterday. They have no other information. I have her Uncle's address.
> She would have come home.
> The neighbours have not seen her.
> Edwyn, she would have come home! You know she is like her father!
> They found no one else. I ...
> She would have come home... There must ... a basement!

The man shouts in English.

> Bertram! There must be a basement.

Rob Morgan looks up and begins to run along the street. He shouts.

> This way.

The police and the workmen turn and follow: running. They disappear down an alley and head for the back of the shops.

****

Edwyn sits in a wooden chair in the corner of the ward where he has been sitting intermittently for the last two weeks. There are four beds, all with patients in various stages of stable but critical illnesses. In the bed nearest to him lies a young woman, her left leg in plaster, her upper torso in a spica cast. She appears asleep. Her chart states she is comatose. Periodically Edwyn leaves his chair, stands beside the girl's bed, and places his hand on her forehead, her arms and nods. He also walks from bed to bed holding his hands above the patient's wounds. He talks to the man nearest the door, who has third degree burns to most of what is left of his body, his legs having been amputated. The man gradually falls asleep and Edwyn returns to his chair.

During the days while he sits, nurses enter, re-position patients, check and re-new intravenous drips or monitor pulses and temperatures. Doctors come and go with students. Sometimes visitors stay a while. They take no notice of Edwyn. On some days, it is Charles who sits there; sometimes both are there to re-position, massage, and feed her. This they accomplish by raising the bed at one end onto blocks. The broth is what Edwyn calls, Sleeper's Gruel.

During the third week, Edwyn, and Charles remove the plaster on the girl's leg. They gently re-position the leg and then apply a new plaster bandage. The girl moans quietly and opens her eyes. Edwyn smiles, Charles turns away.

> *That is much better, is it not Sarah?*
> *Yes, thank you.*
> *Back to sleep then.*
>
> *Edwyn ...*
> *We do not despair, remember?*
> *Those X-Rays.*
> *Remember her father, standing up against Black Shirts, dying as an English soldier on the Normandy beaches. Her mother surviving all she did to get here. Sarah is made from - what your father would have called - good breeding stock. Do not concern. Comb her hair properly boy!*

****

Edwyn is sitting next to the bed when she finally awakens. He tells her not to try moving yet. It is then that Sarah learns of the night her mother died. He tells her what has happened to her, of what must happen now and what might be her immediate future. He tells her that her father's brother Michael has arranged her mother's funeral for when she revives. She tells him that she is no longer a Jew.

> *You cannot erase what you are Sarah.*
> *I can try.*

He turns as two men enter with a stretcher.

> *Sarah, this is Karl and Bertram. Karl is a fireman and Bert is a*
> *policeman. We take you to the ceremony. You will be fine.*
> *There are friends there with Michael's family. Then, we take*
> *you to another hospital in the country. There, you will be able*
> *to begin your convalescence. They are expecting you. The*
> *hospital is good.*

She says nothing. They slide a wooden sliver beneath her and lift her onto the stretcher. Before they go, Edwyn checks the other patients, adjusts a saline drip and places his hands over the burns of his new friend. He tells him that he will visit him again and the man nods.

****

Edwyn, Charles and Bertram are sitting on a bench under a tree in the grounds of Stoke Mandeville Hospital in Aylesbury. It is a cool November day and they are sharing some thermos tea and scones, which Bertram has brought. They are watching patients in wheelchairs practising archery. Sarah is there, being taught how to hold the bow and insert arrows. She keeps dropping the arrows and is the subject of much teasing from other archers.

She seems to be getting on well with the men.
Nurse Clarke says she does get on well with them. They
consider her war-wounded, so she belongs with them. She also
plays wheelchair croquet.
So, Sarah is returning to life. Prognosis Edwyn?
Her spine is still badly injured, but improving. She will, I think,
have a permanent limp. Nurse says she has managed a few
steps. As her strength returns, this will improve. It will take
time. She is intent on leaving the country.
I can understand that. Does she say where?
"Somewhere where I can disappear."
There are already many Jewish people on the move and there
will be more after the Partition Plan. In six months, it will be
the end of the Mandate.
So ends the Balfour Declaration. Now we have a Partition Plan
next week. Is Israel the answer, Bert?
It may not be the answer, but it will happen.
Not for Sarah though. She wants to leave her ancestry behind.
Can one ever do that?

When do you have to have the police car back, young man?
We have another hour yet. I am going to have a little talk with
Nurse Clarke. She has some interesting ideas on criminality!
Always eager to learn. Know what you're thinking Charlie Boy.

I shall sit in the vehicle Edwyn. Michael has asked me to report
back on Sarah. Suggest the idea of America or Australia to her.
We have friends who can help her settle. It would be a new
start for her.
I will. Your Australian plans are progressing?
As any plans can. A new country with opportunity. The men
are optimistic and like Sarah, want to leave the past behind.
You know you have my support, always.
Bless you brother.

They laugh. It is a gentle laugh, their hands touching.

The RMS Strathaird: 1948

14th May

Sarah has found a quiet spot on the starboard deck beneath the lifeboats. She sits in a comfortable chair with cushions ensuring comfort. Her wheelchair and walking stick are within reach. Her book lies upturned on her lap. They have just passed Fayed in the Suez Canal and she watches people on the shore.

There has been increased tension on board since entering the canal. The officers and crew seemed more in view. She noticed that British passengers still enjoyed the sun, games and singing, but those from other parts of Europe, sought out quiet corners. Yesterday, not knowing she was behind the deck door, she had heard one of the officers say he would be glad when they were through the canal and beyond the Red Sea.

Charles is below decks in the Medical Centre. Although the Centre has had a re-fit along with the rest of the ship, the long aisle with buck beds remains as a reminder of the Straithaird's war service. Charles has made one of the bunks his, the one above being taken up with his luggage, portable gramophone, books and typewriter. He is at present (having treated an eight-year boy for a minor head wound) emphasising to his mother that he wishes to see the boy on the morrow, that he must not play any more football at present and that if he vomits or is dizzy to return him at once to the Centre. When he is free, he will change into his white deck shoes, white slacks, and white blazer. With his Panama hat and sunglasses donned, he will go in search of Sarah.

He does the rounds of the decks observing her empty chair and wheelchair from stairs on the deck above. He finds her in the lounge listening with many others to the BBC Home Service relaying David Ben-Gurion's speech, declaring the establishment of Eretz-Israel to be known as the State of Israel. Remaining near the door, he sees her reach for a chair, her face endeavouring to hide pain, her walking stick helping to ease her slowly to rest. People are asking questions, wanting a translation. He sees her get caught up translating in Yiddish for a family. An officer standing near, turns to him.

> *There will be a war don't you think Doc?*
> *It seems likely.*
> *Separation was a bad idea.*
> *The Jewish people want to return to what they regard as their promised land.*
> *A promise that was made a long while ago.*
> *A promise has no limit on time.*

****

6th June

Yesterday, the RMS Straithaird left Colombo. Sarah is watching the sun on the expanse of the Indian Ocean while Charles watches her occasionally from a deck window. He is writing letters.

A man and a woman with two boys turn onto the deck. The boys carry small union jack flags, obviously coming from the D-Day service. They watch Sarah as she fits an arrow to her bow, the woman putting her fingers to her lips to silence the boys. Sarah sends an arrow out into the sea where it arches high, disappears for a second in the sun and seems to slow in its descent into the water. When the arrow disappears, the boys clap their hands.

Sarah turns and laughs, shrugs and lowers herself into her wheelchair. The family move to her and Charles moves closer to the window as she explains how the bow works, holds it against the father to show its height, pings the string for them, and shows them an arrow. The boys are eager to see her shoot again but she shakes her head signifying she only has one last arrow. She pauses and there is discussion. From her holdall, she takes a knife, some hemp and the boys hand their paper flags to her and watch as she binds their thin wooden sticks to her arrow.

She stands hopping on one leg initially, takes the bow from the father, ushers the boys to her side, then steadying herself, she draws the bow back, leans a little backward and releases the arrow. The arch is lower than before, but the sun is there as the arrow and union jacks race towards the water. The arrow hits the water at a perfect 90 degrees and for a moment, the flags seem to float and then are gone.

There is much clapping from the boys and the father shakes Sarah's hand. Charles hears the women talk of tea; Sarah gathers her bag, hands the bow to the eldest boy, the empty quiver to the youngest, swings herself round and settles into her wheelchair and they move away along the deck.

****

12th June

Charles has said farewell to colleagues in the Medical Centre, gathered his belongings together and is in the ballroom writing. It is a letter to join those already addressed and stamped on the table. He finishes addressing the envelope and holds it to lips for a moment before placing it top of the others. He turns as an officer enters the ballroom.

> *They are here, Andrew?*
> *They most certainly are.*

Sarah is sitting in her wheelchair watching the excitement as passengers make their way from the ship. Passengers not leaving have crowded along the upper decks to catch a sight of Fremantle. As those leaving begin to thin out; Sarah watches two men leaving with suitcases, one carrying a gramophone with a large wooden speaker horn. She notices they do not follow the other passengers into the Customs shed but walk along the quay towards a Holden utility where three men greet them with hugs and much laughter. A dog in the back of the vehicle barks with excitement.

Later Sarah leaves, walking with the aid of her walking stick, while an officer follows with her wheelchair. When seated, she turns and waves to people still watching from the decks. Many wave back. The officer begins to push her towards Cliff Street and The Esplanade Hotel.

****

14th June

Charles is sitting in the passenger seat of the utility reading. Richard has his legs over the steering wheel, his eyes closed. Andrew is in the tray behind playing cards with Wilhelm and Stephane. They are parked, back from the harbour, near Cantonment Hill where they have a good view of the Straithaird. Andrew turns and knocks on the back window.

> *Twenty minutes Charles.*
> *Yes, I am watching.*

Much of the morning activity on the Straithaird has ceased and there is just the one lower access to the ship where two sailors are talking. They turn as Sarah's wheelchair stops in front of them. She hands them papers and they prepare to help her with the chair but she stops them. She stands, retrieves her walking stick, and walks onto footbridge. She turns and speaks with one of the sailors who is about to follow with the chair. He laughs and puts his hands in the air leaving the chair on the dockside, then follows her onto the footbridge.

The Straithaird sounds one long blast. The remaining sailor begins to detach the footbridge, looking and up and laughing as Andrew runs up to help him. They walk onto the ship and bring the footbridge in, leaving the wheelchair on the docksides.

There is laughter and banging on the roof of the Holden.

Did he make it?
Just about. I think she is heading for Adelaide.
I did think though, she would stay here.
She booked in for a week and a ticket to Geraldton.
It was a ruse. She just wants to escape Edwyn and
forget the past.
Andrew will see her settled. Then it is up to her is it not?
He was looking forward to seeing Somerset Downs.
And so am I. It is a long drive I believe. I hope, Buddy,
you know how to drive this very strange vehicle.
Hold on to your hat Mon frère.

On the RMS Straithaird, Andrew, now in uniform, is talking to the Captain on the bridge as it heads out into Gage Roads. Sarah is sitting in a first class berth looking at a map of Adelaide.

Part Four

Somerset Downs, Western Australia 2015 -

The Play

The girl was sitting on the right hand side of the cinema. Everyone, including the man who was watching her had chosen seats in the centre, mainly towards the back. As he watched, she reached into a bag, took out a container, extracted and began to eat a sandwich. Now and again she would look up at the advertisements for coming programs from The Metropolitan Opera, National Theatre and Old Vic, particularly seeming to take in the details of David Stratton's lectures on Australian cinema which he was currently giving. He saw her produce a pen and note the dates (he presumed this was what she was doing) on the back of her program for Saint Joan which she had been reading in between the advertisements.

He had to stop his perusal as just before the lights went down, she stopped eating and looking at the screen to turn and look at the others in the audience. He stayed looking at his program until the lights darkened bringing that hush which happens at the beginning of a film or play ensued.

Throughout the play he occasionally looked at her and saw her attention never waver. At the interval, he sat whilst that inevitable murmur came from the audience and was accompanied by moves for coffee or the need to move. The girl just sat looking at the countdown on the screen which showed the National Theatre's Donmar Warehouse audience who like those in this cinema were moving to the aisles.

He wondered what she might be thinking. Was she thinking about that theatre on the screen: those talking who remained seated; the play itself, the actors? Was she wondering whether the Jones' design worked or that Shaw would have been horrified? Would she, like him, wish that modern directors would not try to re-write the plays they were directing to impose their own ideas on the audience.

He had watched her all this time and it was not until the countdown reached 5 mins and the audience was beginning to return that she moved. He was surprised at how well she moved on her crutches and he watched her leave surprised at her speed. He was possessed of the need to see if she was able to manipulate the foyer, whether she was able to negotiate the doors and steps. It was an effort for him to remain seated and so he moved.

She was talking to the young man making a coffee. He turned, putting the lid on the cup and asked her if she could manage.

I'm fine, thank you.

She gently began placing the cup in a pocket in her cardigan and turned.

Here let me carry that for you

He held his hand out to take the cup.

No. Thanks. I'm fine.

He followed her negotiating the two steps up to the doors, held them open for her for which she thanked him once more, and then watched as she carefully walked in rhythm with the crutches to her seat, making the next act with half a minute to spare.

When the performance ended she was one of the few who accompanied those in the Donmar clapping. Like her he sat watching them take their bows and wondered if like him, she would have preferred to have been there, in London, surrounded by that audience.

He knew she would wait until the audience had left before leaving her seat, so he waited in the foyer, casually picking up flyers for films he would not see. She saw him immediately she had pushed open the doors and come through. He smiled and she gave him a beginning smile then sat in one of the coloured chairs totally unsuited to the clientele who frequented this cinema. Perhaps, he thought, she was waiting for someone to join her, but realised that it was to wait until most of the groups deciding where they would go, had left.

He watched her gather her crutches and head for the doors where she used her back to push, keep open and step outside them. He smiled at the way she adjusted the crutches, her hat, handbag, and then moved to the traffic lights to wait. He saw her begin to cross, taking her time although the red light flashed. He caught up to her as she stopped at the doors to the Dome and said.

> *Allow me.*
> *Ah. I should hire you as my door-opener.*
> *It would be a pleasure.*

He was pleased this made her laugh. They moved to the counter where someone was ordering.

> *What did you think of Arterton?*
> *She was fine I thought, but ...*
> *You did not appreciate the modern dress?*
> *Not so much that. I do not like directors and producers altering text. There is no need to do that with Shaw.*
> *The text unsullied?*
> *Definitely.*

He listened as she ordered her scrambled eggs, no bread and Orange Pekoe tea, noted she already had twenty dollars in a pocket to hand to the young man, watched as she popped her number stand under arm and head towards the bench sofas. As he ordered he wondered if today was enough or whether he could push his contact with her beyond this.

> *May I join you?*
> *You already have your hand on the chair.*
> *May I?*
> *I cannot pay much for a door opener.*
> *Totally free – whenever. Charles Fairfield Moorehouse at your service.*

Please sit Mr. Moorehouse.

As he sat he was aware of the strain beneath the mask with which she faced the world. He wanted to say: hold on, do not give up, I can help.

> *And you?*
> *Me Mr Moorehouse? Sarah Townsend, the girl with crutches.*
> *So, you approve of Arterton?*
> *Yes, but would it not have been wonderful to see Sybil Thorndike as Joan?*
> *Most certainly,* he said remembering. *He wrote it for her.*
> *Yes, I know.*
> *You are obviously a Shavian.*
> *No membership, but certainly a Shavian. I have some of his plays on DVD.*
> *You have a favourite?*
> *Ah, so many. Possibly Man and Superman. Did you see Fiennes in it?*
> *Yes I did. It was quite something.*
> *One could easily fall for Fiennes.*

They both laughed and he smiled at his thoughts of her falling in love. One could certainly fall in love with someone who would have liked to see Sybil Thorndike. When their orders came he watched her eat and wished he had ordered more than just a croissant and coffee.

> *I have Obsession in my diary to see. Will you be coming to see that?*
> *Maybe. It looks rather dark and dismal.*
> *And Saint Joan wasn't?*
> *You have me there.*

There was an element of self-deprecation in her that he liked.

> *Do you know Back to Methuselah?*
> *Yes. Never seen it of course. He did not write it for the stage.*
> *I believe, although, it has been staged.*

A Washington theatre staged it earlier this year.

She looked up and paused.

You are going to tell me you saw it, aren't you?

Careful, he thought. How did she do that? Not too fast.

I was there for a Convention. Methuselah was a plus. I think you would have enjoyed it. It is great fun in parts.
Do you believe what Shaw suggests?

And this is where you may definitely lose her, he thought. I should have done this some other way. Take a breath.

Lamarck over Darwin's evolution you mean?
Cannot one think both might be right and have their place?
I agree.
Ah Mr. Moorehouse. We live in a world that does not want to think about whether we can improve ourselves and become wiser. It is left to those who think history matters. Oh, to live for a thousand years. Would that not be fun? Just think what one could do.

He looked down at his coffee which he was sure was cold. If you go ahead with this, she will cause you much happiness and grief. She will suffer by your side and you now know, with certainty, that whatever she says to the contrary, she will be loyal.

Yes, it is something on which to ponder. Ms Sarah Townsend, I must be going. Thank you for allowing me to open doors for you. Perhaps we shall meet at the showing of Obsession?
Perhaps.

She smiled and he held out his hand which she took. She held it and smiling said.

You have such an Anglo-Welsh sounding name
Mr Moorehouse. Moorehouse? I think you are neither. A hint
of French?
You are right. Long ago, however. Now an Australian Citizen
and door opener.
Good to talk with you Mr. Moorehouse.
And you Ms. Townsend.

He knew she would watch which way he turned and wait a while. He knew their meeting would concern her and would add to the many fears in her life. And he knew they could not wait until the showing of *Obsession*.

A Marriage

It had been a couple of years since I had been to the city and I was surprised at the number of cranes intent on new buildings when it is supposed to be hard to raise money. We were staying at one of the plush hotels and taking up nearly the whole floor. The marriage was to take place there and we had a suite large enough to hold the celebration.

I think all marriages need to be a celebration but this one was a little sad although we were all looking forward to it. After all, we had not had a marriage for so many moons and we all hoped that this one would bring children and happiness. It was to be, as Charles said, something to remember: a turn point. I was not sure.

For me, it was a rush. Well for all of us. For we did not know this was to happen. Just a week before we knew. And so they were to be married. I liked Sarah from the beginning. She was kind and shy. She always wore clothes from long past and to the floor. Pretty they were. I remember she asked me one morning where in Albania I came from. When I told her, she had even travelled through Lezhë and knew Lac: my place. She said she wanted to see Kosovo and Albania after the war. It is a beautiful country Stephane, she said. Sometimes in a country like this, it would be good again to visit with my old village, but there is nothing for me there. And also, I have spent so many years in other places, so memories of Lac are from another time. A remembered sadness.

The ceremony was in the morning, sun shining through the high windows and a view over the lovely Swan River. There were flowers and everything seemed very quiet. It was a lady who married them, very strange to me, but she was welcoming and spoke to everyone before, so it was a cheery feeling. I could see though that Charles wanted everything to go smoothly: as always. Richard looked happy. We have so long seemed to have left the making legal of marriages but he wanted this one to be legal, at least in Australia.

I cry at funerals but I also find it hard not to cry at weddings and I wished we had been in a church: any church. Churches always make me cry. Patrice looked at me, smiled and gave me a shoulder hug. I thought he had a tear as well. I think we were all to hope this would be a good marriage and that our hopes become real.

And so it was over and we had no time for celebration - that had to be later - because Charles had organised meetings. We all thanked the celebrant lady and she left. Charles was fussing over Sarah, Richard, of course, as well. She waved her hand and said, "Let's go." And so we did, Daniele in charge of Sarah's chair, Richard at her side talking.

The next stop was our lawyers. Charles and Richard knew them well but Mr. Campbell Senior usually came up to The Downs with papers to sign. Their offices looked from a Victorian time but with much light. Both the Campbell men were there and there was much shaking of hands. We had not been told why we were there but thought it was to do with the marriage. But it was also to hear that Richard had changed his will.

So we heard that Sarah was to be his beneficiary at his death which did not come as a surprise. What did come though as a surprise was that Sarah was to be gifted Somerset Downs at once. This was why Richard explained, he wanted us all to be there. This was also a surprise to Sarah.

> *But I do not want it. You must not do this. That wasn't …*

Richard stopped her.

> *It is a present Sarah. A marriage present. One does not refuse a marriage present.*

There was a silence. I saw Josiah smile and shrug his shoulders. And then Daniele said,

> *You cannot refuse Sarah. It's a present.*
> *But it is your home!*

Yours too Sarah, said Richard*, and I know you will take care of it.*

We could see she was cross but resigned. There was a slight cough from Mr. Campbell.

We need these to be signed Richard and you Charles, to witness the change in ownership and beneficiary. You also Mark, as attorney.

We watched as the signings were carried out. I watched Bill and Patrice chatting and Daniele adjusting the cover on Sarah's knees. Josiah and Gregor were appraising the Campbell's paintings and me: did any of this concern me? Perhaps that The Downs was now Sarah's, but somehow I knew things would not change that much and contemplating the future was never anything that gave me cause for to be concerned.

Fine, all done. It was Charles.
Not quite. There is the business of Ms Townsend's will for her to sign. I am not sure if you want the details to be known Ms. Townsend?
Yes, please Mr. Campbell.

I shall never forget Charles' face. Richard's was just surprise, but Charles' was not only surprise. I could see him almost stamping his foot in irritation. He was so used to knowing and being Les Majesté. It was good to see he had, perhaps, met his match.

Mr Campbell then read that on Sarah death, all her properties and monies were to be divided equally between Richard and any children. Should she survive Richard, their children were to be equal sharers. Should she survive Richard and there be no children, all property and monies were to be gifted to Charles. I saw Charles look first at Sarah and then Richard.

Thank you Mr. Campbell. I need to sign that I think.

We watched as Daniele pushed Sarah to the desk and they helped her sign, with Mr. Mark and Mr. Ross witnesses.

At least I can still sign my name.

She laughed. No-one else, of course, did. But Patrice got up and bent over and kissed Sarah on the cheek.

As they say here: Good on you Sarah.
Yes Sarah. And Daniele added his kiss.

So we all moved over to cheek-kiss Sarah and the atmosphere became merry. Even Charles, who was the last, moved over and took her hand.

Well done, my dear.
I think we have another port of call Charles?

It was obvious that Sarah did not know exactly where we were to go and was surprised it was a bank. This time the offices were of what is called I think: the now. All new, bright colours and uncomfortable chairs. Only Richard, Sarah and Daniele, who insisted on pushing Sarah, because *"he was the best wheelchair pusher in Australia,"* went into the office. It was not until later when he told us that Sarah had been cross because Richard had given her "pots" of money which she refused and which – apparently – she already had because he had arranged it.

So that day, on her marriage day, Sarah became one of us. Someone who had property and money. It is a guarantee and insurance, although not one on which to rely. She has since become my very dear and loving friend. She is dear to me as any daughter and I would give my life for her without a moment's thinking.

70

Travelling

I was about to get a spa room ready for the next appointment when Peter rang from the office to say there was a new lady who might need help as she could not walk. She had her own therapist. I would just be needed to assist and perhaps give a massage. He had cleared me for a two hour session.

The girl was in a wheelchair and obviously not well. Her husband said all he needed was help in moving her on the table so as not to hurt her. He explained he was a therapist and there was a particular type of therapy his wife was having closely related to Reiki. This was when I first met Sally and Richard who stayed for about two months at the resort.

They were lovely people and I would see them sometimes three times a day. I found out that he was actually a doctor as well and he specialised in motor neurone diseases. He was patient with Sally and she was so good because it must have been tedious to go through all he and she did for hours each day.

When I came on duty they would already be in the pool. At the beginning he would carry her down into the shallow end and then just pull her along until he had to swim, and she would just float behind. All the time though, he would be talking to her. He never seems to stop talking even when she was in the spa. We would make sure she was comfortable and wrapped in towels and he would spend some time just holding the sides of her head, then move to her arms and legs just placing his hands on them. It was so sad because she looked so frail with no hair, her eyes so huge. He would be talking about anything and everything. He would spend some time on current news items in the morning but mostly he would talk about books, art, and history: anything. He knew a lot and I learned so much: believe me.

Sometimes though, he would speak in another language. He assured me – not to say anything that I could not hear – but that Sally was learning Russian and believe it or not, Welsh. I did wonder why anyone would bother given her predicament. When they first came, she would mainly just listen or occasionally ask, "Why was that", or "I don't understand." Gradually though as she seemed to have less pain, she would talk more. I came to admire her because she never once complained and it must have been hard because Richard just kept on to his timetable with the pool and the table. Always reading to her or talking.

I remember him reading *Moby Dick* to her and although I vaguely knew the story, I had forgotten or did not know why they were whaling. There was so much about the way people lived then and how everyone needed the oil for lighting. All those whales killed for light. My mother used to come up for weekends sometime and I remember going home and asking if she knew where Nantucket was because I never did until that day. I was full of the life lived then and told her what I had been hearing. Just imagine: the world so dark as it used to be then and how life was so hard.

They had been with us for about a month and I was beside the pool waiting for him to finish when I heard her laugh and then Richard with a "Yes!" Sally was just floating on her own but not only that, she was moving her arms to steady herself. Then she began to move forward on her own with just a slow movement of her legs doing dog paddle. It was just a few strokes and he was there supporting her but you could see how happy he was.

And so Sally slowly improved. It was slow, you could hardly notice but after another month she was doing the paddle on her own and he was supporting her from behind as she used the crutches. She was also able to negotiate her chair and I remember seeing him running behind her early one morning as she raced around the pool at top speed. And that is when they left for the first time.

Richard said they needed to move further north and they were planning to go over the top end. Sally said she thought they would be back later in the year. Richard was so good to us all and I know Peter and the staff were sorry to see them go. We all wished them well on their journey. Peter thought it was just a fluke, her improvement, and that she could not possible survive. It was just false hope. He had seen it before. I knew what he meant.

But they did return and I was glad I was still there when they came back because I had been thinking of returning to Perth, which I eventually did. It was so good to see them and to see Sally walk in with new hair – not a wig – and smiling at my surprise. Richard was slightly behind her and it was Sally who booked them in, separate rooms again, Peter trying not to act as if this was unusual.

If I thought things would be different this time, they were not. Well they were the same but also different. Peter immediately cancelled my appointments to make the days clear for them as before because that was what Richard particularly wanted. I was so pleased because they were always a delight to work for. This time I was able to do more massage and Sally really liked having the stones and foot massages. It was also good to see how Richard was content to have her say what she wanted, but basically he worked much the same.

In the pool though, things were different. It was hard to remember how he used to carry her into the pool. Now Sally was there ready for him at the side and they would both dive in and swim lengths: so many lengths. Me, I love to swim but the lengths they used to do! Three or four times a day. It was obvious he paced her and would not let her go faster than he wished. They would swim so many lengths freestyle, back stroke, breast and then lengths just using legs and then arms. It was a real workout.

Then after showering Sally would come to me for a massage. Always gentle where she would sometimes go to sleep. I would put the hot stones where Richard wanted them and just do Swedish massage on her back and legs. He would never leave her with me, just sit and read until we were finished. In fact I never ever saw them other than together.

Peter said though he thought one day they had quarrelled. Peter seemed to have forgotten their previous visit and when I told him, he thought Richard pushed her too hard and that she might relapse. He said this day Richard had requested a heat pillow for his arm which he had injured and that was why they were not using the pool or my services. Peter, who always thought the worst of anything, thought Richard was lying. Anyway they obviously made it up, if that was what it was, because they were there at dinner, talking as usual.

When they left, they said they were going home which was somewhere in the wheat belt. Richard though, knew I was thinking of leaving, and gave me an address of a place in Wanneroo which is where I now work: senior position. Lovely place, all the most modern equipment you could wish for and good money. The best is I see Sally sometimes who comes in for "the works" as she calls it. She has also introduced us to many of her friends. Mostly farmer's wives who book in for a "girl's spa day." I can hardly remember what Sally used to be like when I first saw her. She is Richard's miracle.

The Engagement Ring

She was scrunched up in the bed trying to remember what it was like before but the awakening terror of it all overshadowed memory. It had never been a pain and here it was again, that abdominal heaviness, ache and cramp.

The alarm clock said it was time but instead of the normal reaction to these hands and the pulsating second hand, she pulled her doona tight around her covering the growing light from around the blinds and lay for another full minute before throwing the doona back, running to the door, finding the "Do Not Disturb" sign, opening the door, placing it on the handle, then closing and locking the door. Retreating to the bed, she again buried herself in the covers and groaned. Gradually the warmth grew and despite the dull aches, she dozed.

She awoke to feel him watching her and turned her head.

> *How did you get in here? Didn't you see the sign?*
> *Yes, of course. You kept me waiting at the pool. Up you get.*
> *There is still time before breakfast.*
> *How did you get in here? I locked the door.*
> *Do you really think a locked door would stop me? I thought you were ill.*
> *Well I am.*
> *What you have is not an illness Sarah. It will help you to swim.*

He knew, as she glared at him, that this again, was where he had to be careful.

> *I am having a day off.*
> *We do not have days off. You know that.*
> *I am not moving from this bed.*
> *Swimming will help.*
> *How do you know what will help?*
> *I may not be a woman, but I am not ignorant of these experiences.*

Experiences! Go away!

He turned and left. Immediately she felt guilty and was tempted to shower, to dress and to swim. But she lay, almost luxuriating in this renewal and remembering from long ago when she had been familiar with what was happening to her. She had never resented her monthly and now lay thinking that again her life had changed. This was a transition: becoming what she had once been. She knew that instead of being angry with him, she should have thanked him.

The door opened and he was holding a wheat bag.

> *They have heated this up and it should help with the*
> *pain. Don't fuss. I apparently have tennis elbow. Do you want*
> *it?*
> *Thanks.*
> *See you in an hour.*
> *I'm having a day off.*
> *See you in an hour.*

When she awoke, she could see from the light framing the blinds that it was past mid-day. She turned and saw him sitting in the armchair, legs crossed in the way he did, reading.

> *It must be afternoon.*

He looked up.

> *Yes, it is.*
> *You did not wake me.*
> *You said you were having a day off.*
> *You said, see you in an hour.*
> *Yes I did.*
> *And?*
> *Decided to have a day off.*
> *Very funny. Go away.*
> *Sure you are fine? Want another wheat bag?*

Go away.

Later, when she felt refreshed from a leisurely shower, had dressed, and eaten a room service lunch, she smiled thinking this day was special. I will now, hopefully, be able to have children. The thought, put away for so long, almost frightened her. It was not just a hope. What was Charles always saying about hope? And she agreed. It must happen. I will have children. I will keep my part of the bargain.

Although she felt she was missing the routine, she decided to enjoy the rest of her day off and headed for the beach. She was aware of everything around her: the sea, the birds, the sand, the grass outcrops on the dunes, the sound her sandshoes made in the wet sand, the gentle flop of the end of a wave. All this surrounded her and she felt her body glowed with warmth so welcome she wanted to cry out. She wanted to share this new feeling. She wanted to: what did she want?

Sitting at the edge of a rock pool she knew the tears were there but let them dry in the wind, knew that whatever happened now would change the routine, the plans, the way perhaps he treated her. Would the plans change? How much time did she have? Could she just up and disappear? Throw the future to the winds?

She saw him walk from the dunes to the strand about a couple of miles away. I am not going to move. I will not go to meet him. He can just turn and go back. But she knew he would not do this. Knew he would have seen her and knew that he would just walk casually towards her. She watched him the whole way. When he arrived, he did not smile.

> *Room on that rock for me?*
> *Have you had tea?*
> *Yes. Strange without you.*
> *Lonely?*
> *No, just strange.*

They settled into a silence, hearing the birds, both watching the sea and the fading of the day.

I have a present for you.
A present?
Something I think I forgot to give you, or at the time it did not seem to be relevant, but it has been something I have wished to amend. Not really a present I suppose.
Intriguing.

He smiled and reached for her hand.

I found this a while back and thought of you because it has Celtic scrolls around the stones. I just liked it and hope you do as well. I am not sure how one arranges this, whether this now will go first or second, but I thought it could be an engagement ring as you do not have one. A bit late I know, but I think women like to have engagement rings. I know you say "posh" to such things, but I thought it wrong that you did not have one. So please accept this.

There was no box, no getting down on knees, no champagne, no kiss, but a gentle pressing of the ring onto her marriage finger to join the gold band. She bit her lips. I will not cry she thought.

It is lovely. Thank you Richard. Very kind of you and very thoughtful.
Glad you like it. Dinner?

The Ward

When I came to, I realised I was in hospital. There was a pain in the side of my head and I still had that headache. I remember the headache.

The light in the ward was low and I thought it might be night or evening. I could hear some music though. A piano. I moved slightly and realised I had a drip in my arm and that is when I saw the girl turning towards me from the X-rays she was looking at.

> *Ah. You are awake. Hallo Eddie. I'm Sarah.*
> *You're a nurse?*
> *Yes, I suppose I am, among other things.*
> *You been riding?*
> *Well I have. Just popped in to see how you were faring. I will let the Big Man know you are awake.*
> *Big Man?*
> *Doctor Charles.*
> *Where am I?*
> *This is First Aid Eddie. Well, that's what we call it. Because, mostly it is first aid, but then sometimes, it is a little more. In your case: a little more, than First Aid. I'll go get the Big Man.*

And she disappeared. A Riding Nurse. The next thing seemed to be a dream. I remember dreaming I was at home in New South Wales, and seeing my mum, but she was sounding like my dad. Then there was the girl again but there were a couple of guys. Nobody looked like doctors and the girl was now in shirt and shorts. I thought I was going on a picnic.

> *How are you old chap?* Said one of the guys.

He sounded far away, like underground. The other guy was shining a torch in my eyes, holding my eyes open.

> *Am I okay?*

Well, you have done some damage. None of which is beyond repair. One broken arm and you hit your head as you fell which has you concussed. That should heal and we are about to re-set your arm which as you can see is in a rather make-shift splint at present. Richard here has sent for your wife who is picking your bairns up and will be here shortly. Questions?
What happened?
Well you were in the low meadow paddock with Bill. You became ill and jumped from the windrower. Not an easy thing to do. Bumped your head, broke your arm and here you are.

This from the other guy.

Yes, the windrower. I had a headache. There was a light. So hot I couldn't see.

And then the other one said.

Yes. You also had a grand mal Eddie. Which is why you should not have been on any machinery. We need to have a talk about that. You are very lucky. You have Sarah to thank as she saw you when riding down to the Gate House.

Then the Riding Nurse said,

Need to give you something Eddie, while we deal with your arm. Just make you a bit more woosey than you already are.

She was a strange nurse. And that was that. When I came too again, there was Nancy.

Hi Nance.
You bloody pillock.
What?
You think they will keep you on now? This is a dry place Ed!

And she just looked that look she gives me. One that says she has had enough. One that says she may pack up and leave.

> *I knew this was a dry place and I didn't drink. It was just that*
> *headache. I am so thirsty.*
> *We can fix that.*

And there was the Riding Nurse with the kids. They thought my cast great and said could they draw on it. The Riding Nurse girl said maybe tomorrow, your dad has to get some sleep. Clive asked me if I was okay and little Stace wanted to get up to kiss me, so Clive gave her a leg up. Then they went off with the Riding Nurse to see if dinner was ready. Nance stayed but I daren't look at her.

> *They said you will be okay. But you had a fit.*
> *It must have been the headache. It was killing me.*

I know it began just after Bill's mate Chris picked me up. When we met up with Bill, I signed all the forms, and took some Panadol. By lunch time we had met the other guys, eaten and went our different ways around the place. Some were helping to build the new quarters. Bill said it was going to be like the Hilton when finished and laughed. I seem to have been popping Panadol all day because that headache never lifted and in the morning it was worse. Suppose I should have told him. But I had just begun work. Couldn't do it.

Nance told me they had all been nice and that they were going to put them up for the night again. She said the place was like a hotel. The Doc had been asking questions though about where I worked before and why I left.

> *Told him you had been laid off from the mine and finding it*
> *hard to get something.*
> *They might pay me for at least a day.*
> *You think!*

I knew she would be feeling that again I was out of work. Thought this was a break. Bill was good taking me on when one of them had to go east. I was trying to work out if I had seen anything else on the boards before this when the Doc came back. The Riding Nurse was with him and told Nance that dinner was being served and would she like to come.

> I'll make sure that Eddie has something. Don't worry. He really needs to ret up.

So Nance went and I was left with the Doc Charles. This guy did not pull punches.

> So how much alcohol do you generally put away in a day Eddie?
> I...
> You could lie if it makes you feel better.
> A fair bit I suppose. But I can stop when I like.
> Can you? Well your body says: no you cannot. Stop that is. That is what happened to you. You went into withdrawals.
> Nancy has me going to AA.
> That is never going to help you. May help some. Not you.
> I can stop.
> Do you want to?
> Course.
>
> Not the right answer Eddie. Do you want your wife to leave you? Do you want those rather well-mannered children of yours to grow up with a drunk for a father?
> Hey!
> Well Eddie. Do you? Think about the answer your wife would like to hear. We'll talk again.

And that was that because he was gone again. And I must have been too. When I came around again, I asked how long I had been in hospital. I realised their answers were putting me off. The Riding Nurse was good at this. Ask the Doc she would say, but he never seemed to be around.

I think it was the next day I saw Nance again with that Riding Nurse. She looked much less angry with me. I told her I was sorry and that I would have a try at those other jobs.

> *Not to worry. I think they might keep you on.*

This was more than a surprise given what the Doc said when I last saw him.

> *The kids are fine. They are having a grand time in the pool and one of the men has taken them to see the horses. Greg I think – yes Greg. Richard has shown me around too. They seem to have everything here. It really is a lovely place.*

I said, I thought it was a hospital. And who was Richard? She laughed.

> *He's one of the doctors who saw you. He says all the tests they did on you are okay I think. He'll tell you.*

It was Doc Charles who told me. He said I had had all the tests - could not believe all the equipment they had - the works. The Doc said everything seemed okay. The concussion would remedy itself and there was no damage. I asked him when I could leave but he said that would depend on …

> *On what?*
> *What you are going to do.*
> *Me?*
> *Yes, your future Eddie, and drinking.*
> *That's not your concern mate.*

He was getting really much. I should have known from the way he spoke the last time. I told him that I knew they would not want to keep me on. He agreed. Just kept nodded his flipping head.

> *And this is a dry place.*
> *Mmm*

So if I stay, it's no drink.
It would have to be. It all depends on you and what you want your future to be: and the future of your wife and children.
I want things to change but it has been hard.
Important things always are. I have things to do — talk to you later.

And he was gone. And that is where I was, thinking about Nance, the kids and the time we had our own house and the future looked bright. Remembering these snapshots which I know sounds cuckoo from me but they brought tears. I must have slept because when I looked up the Riding Nurse was there.

Taking you for a walk Eddie.
Where?
Just around. Thought you might like to see the children and join us for dinner.

She brought a wheelchair — no walking — she said. She helped me from the bed. I felt weak. My arm itched like mad. When we left the ward and went through the door we were in the corridor of a house. It looked like my gran's house when I was a kid. The sun was pouring through a coloured window shining on the polished parquet. There were paintings everywhere.

Through here Eddie.

And then we were in what was a huge dining area and kitchen. A different building. Through the windows I could see a pool with my son sitting on the edge. Riding Nurse pushed me to the windows and slid open one of the panels. And we were outside on a patio. I could see Nance in the pool with Stacey. They were both laughing. There was a barbecue with a few guys around it. One was Bill who gave me a wave.

Doc Richard, who seemed nicer than Doc Charles with all the questions, came over.

Thanks Sarah. Are you going to swim?
Sure thing.

And away she went to the side of pool, said something to Clive, and they both jumped into the water.

How are doing Eddie?
The Doc says I am okay. Can I really stay?
Up to you dear chap.
What does that mean?
Well for you, it means never drinking again – ever. Not just here but for the rest of your life. All about that thing called moral fibre Ed.
Moral fibre?
Yes, you hold the future of your family – at this very moment – in your hands. All about moral fibre. Wanting to do something good and doing it.

I liked him better than the Doc Charles, but he made me depressed. My back against a wall. Nance: she was the same. It is up to you Ed. I could hear her saying it. Could I do it I thought?

Don't worry, you'll have help but it all depends on you. Do you want to kick it?
At this moment – more than anything.
But will you?

I could see him smile and I knew this was a moment. Never really liked drinking. The taste of beer was okay. But – what it did to me – how people looked at you when you were even slightly drunk and I was more often really drunk. How pals always seemed to want you to drink more. It had been a nightmare really and here in the sunlight, looking at the men laughing over something, seeing my kids enjoying the pool, seeing Nance smiling again, wouldn't everyone want this?

Yes, I will give it up.
A life time commitment?

Yes and never drink again – from this day on for the rest of my life. I promise myself and anyone who wants to hear.

I saw him look over my head and nod slightly. I guessed it was to the Doc Charles. I turned my head and called to him.

Yes I will.

He came through from the dining room and held out his hand which I took.

This promise is to be totally disconnected to your drinking past. Good for you. You might like to know that Nancy and I have been busy: all with Nancy's agreement. We have arranged for your family to move into another house: she disliked that rental. Clive and Stacey have been enrolled at a nearby school. An excellent one I might add. Nancy has plans to continue her studies which I believe she has had to forego. Okay with you? It is not only your life Eddie.

My world completely changed! I could have easily thrown the wheelchair at him.

You can re-join Bill's team in a couple of days. Very light duties. I think you may be able to help with the motors. I still want you to rest up for a while.
To keep an eye on me?
No Eddie. I am not your jailer but Nancy and the children must have a future.
I know they deserve that but why should you care.
Don't you know?
You didn't meet us until a few days ago. And yes, I know Nance is way above me. She has always been but she chose me, not some uni guy. Me!
And that is why you need to keep your promise. For Nancy, for Clive and for Stacey. I'll leave you with that then …

And he came behind me saying that I needed to move over to the side of the pool to meet up with everyone. So Doc Charles and Doc Richard pushed me over to the barbecue. I joined them talking and listening and watching my family waving from the pool. I was thinking how in such a short time everything seemed to have changed. It was a change I had always wanted, I know, but had never had the guts to do it.

And that is what happened. The removers moved our stuff into the new place over the next few days. The kids started their new school. I had another couple of days being looked after by Sarah, (I will always think of her as The Riding Nurse), to make sure I did not fit again and the fever was gone completely. Then I started work on "light" stuff with Bill. I remember I could not believe this place. Bill said I could move into the quarters as soon as Doc said. And that is what happened and I am now a part of life at The Downs.

Nancy seems to be younger or had I stopped looking at her? Clive and little Stacey love their new school. I do not see the others at the big house much. Charles rides down to see Bill sometimes to "touch base" as Bill says and gives me a wave now and then when he spots me. I have the feeling that he keeps up to date with Nancy and the kids, although they say he does not visit.

There is a part of me that knows what the Doc meant. Nancy has always been on a shelf above me. Clive's going to be the same I think and that is what the Doc saw and why he is interested in my future, because it is theirs as well.

So to date I go with the gang to work on other farms as well as The Downs. We have a four day week would you believe? Clive plays chess with young Dan on Fridays. Stacey is my lovely special girl, just like her Mum. Nancy seems to love me once again and - I have not had a drink for - it must be about eighteen months.

Chess Playing

I became aware of the hush, not silence, but a smooth collective sound of them all breathing. I daren't look up.

Stephane had called dinner in 15 minutes: when was it? Then, I had heard Richard playing from the lounge, Josh discussing some political point with Patrice, rattling the pages of the paper to emphasis his argument. Greg, I know, would have been helping Stephane. Bill would probably be putting away his brushes in the studio. Charles, as always and I didn't need to see, would have the business pages, committing figures to memory. Now they breathed as one, not a sound from the kitch.

Dan didn't look up – he never did.

> So, my lovely girl, you think you can Kasparov me.

It wasn't a question. I swallowed.

> I would not presume. I think though – possibly – my lovely boy, I might be Sarah Townsending you.

I heard – just discernible – an intake of breath and I knew they would be passing their wagers via hand and eye contact. It was Dan's move. He was never this long. And then he moved the Queen's bishop. I thought what *would* Fischer do: what would Spassky do? Keep to your plan Sarah. I knew Dan was thinking along Dan/Spassky lines. No - he was thinking that, Daniele Beniamino Gesualdo had beaten me – yet again.

Then I moved the pawn: I had never lasted this long and I was going to win.

> So – and I could feel the background tension in the room – *you have moved the pawn*, said Dan looking up at me.
> Do you Sarah Helena Townsend realize?
> I have you in three.

You have me in three.

Then they moved. We were surrounded.

> *I can't believe it!*
> *Why not?*
> *What moves?*
> *Sarah – you wonder! Do you know what you have done?*

I looked up at Richard and smiled. He nodded.

> *Well, let's see.*

Then Dan moved his last knight: which he had to do. Then I moved my rook, Check. Dan shrugged and moved his King, and I had him.

> *Come here my lovely girl.* He nearly upset the game getting up.
> *Dan, I am...*

I moved my feet to free myself from Goldie.

> *Do you know no-one has beaten me in ten years? It was the Queen, wasn't it?*
> *I know and yes.*
> *Great fun Sal. Great fun. Did you see that Father?*
> *A worthy opponent I think.*
> *Stephane, a celebration Daniele loses at chess.*
> *Yeah! Stephanade is required.*

I could not escape from Dan's warm body. It was always different hugging Dan. He buried his face in one's shoulder and shook you until you either gave him a sign or Josh touched his arm.

> *Come eat,* called Stephane.

I was glad when everyone was at table and had calmed down a little.

What did you lose?
Three laundries.
Three?
Well, I was just going on form.
Patrice wouldn't wager.
Thank you Pat.

Patrice always had my back. Well, they all did. I knew how privileged I was being the only female.

How many Bill?
Two weedings in the hydros.
Father, did you lose?
No, I won the main house.
You bet against your own magnificent son!
It was the only time I have won!
Richard?
Two weedings and delousing the tomatoes. Sorry Sarah.

And on they went. Charles was quiet, just listening as always. He laughed now and again, whilst Richard just occasionally looked over and smiled at me. He knew I had been at the books and matches for ages and was glad for me.

I knew Sal would win one day. She gnaws at anything until she gets it right. Look at her with the horses. They all want her riding them. Look at Goldie! It is as though that dog can read her thoughts. I mean it!

They all laughed at Patrice, he with his lovely Charles Aznavour cadence. To divert them I said.

Changing the subject. The documentary! Who would have thought that we shall soon have to convert all our vehicles to electric before we then have to convert them to self-drive, or does that mean completely new vehicles?

And they were off! As usual, we had Josh and Dan, the mechanics, knowing more than anyone and saying it would take ages, whilst Charles (and why wouldn't it be Charles?) knew exactly where and to what extent self-drives were actually being made and used now.

By the time Stephane and Greg rose to bring in the dessert, we were back on the banks, which have taken up much discussion this week. We hadn't even got to the latest Trump! I shrunk back into just listening, and feeling just a little, of what my heroes, particularly Fischer, may have felt.

Riding

When I first met Sarah, she looked apprehensive. No: she was scared. Frightened. I have seen it before when reality sets in and people do not know quite how to behave. We all have that sense of things known and when the usual boundaries are stretched beyond comprehension this can break people. Sarah was not broken but she had a look that said: get ready to run if ...

Although it is years since, I still have that feeling that my dear Sally, no matter how she has become one of us, (and she most certainly has): is ready to run. I laugh, because that really applies to all of us. And when have we all not had to run?

All experiencing a time when running was the only thing to do, leaving all behind. We have the bags packed. The Plans A, B and C committed to memory. Everything checked regularly. Nothing left to chance. Knowing of course, that chance always plays its part.

But for me, until recently, my part at The Downs was always transitory. It was meant to be. My place has always been France. Only Sally had made me stay longer. Rick just wanted me to train them all to ride well and this I have achieved. Even Dan rides well now. I pride myself on the saddle I designed for him which now makes him smile, not wince.

Sally would come down every morning. Always trying to be earlier than me, so that she could saddle Beauty by herself. I had liked though to have both horses saddled and ready so that we could enjoy the morning light and what the new day brought. Even in winter, she was there having already swum her lengths. The land, at those times, reminded me of my country where the mists rise from the rivers. Here, the mists seem to rise from the valleys and one can imagine one is somewhere in Europe.

Since everyone came to ride and well, there was little for me to do but exercise the horses, tend to their needs, look after the farrowing/veterinary things which came up and generally be: *le gars cheval*.

It was good though: horses have always been part of my life. I loved riding in a group as we used of old. We would gather at least once in the week usually Thursdays or Fridays morning before weekend departures.

This group ride was good for everyone. And the horses. The dogs would come as well although Greg's *el stuppo* could not make the whole ride and diverted to the homeward trail to wait. Goldie usually made the whole ride, although sometimes if she saw a good jumping point would run ahead and wait for us. She never missed to land in front of Sally who lay back, loosened the reins and had her hand out ready to scoop her in. Beauty never raised a hair, so used she was to this. Those three have always been in tune.

When Sally came down that first morning, she had never ridden, and confessed to being a little "afraid" of horses. She asked me if I would teach her. I knew Rick wanted her to learn but I had never pushed it, neither had he. She just thought she should ride. "If I am staying." I asked – was she? "Not sure yet Patrice. There is commitment you know. We shall see, shall we not? What's your wager?" She laughed. "You see I know! And I know that your wager is very much against me. Even given that: would you teach me?"

So I did. She became someone to challenge Charles and myself and His Majesty takes some beating. I think Sally knows how well she did (I told her so many times), although she just rode like everyone else when we were together. I know though that Charles saw her because I spied him up there on the top hill watching in the early mornings.

I wonder if Sally knows how much her future depended on him. She may think it is Rick but it is really Charles. It is always Charles. When we were *en difficulté,* it was always Charles who knew exactly how to turn situations to our advantage. He seems to have foresight, which of course he denies with rigour. I think Sally has perhaps wormed her way even into the heart of Charles. Even as I think this, I hear another voice saying: not possible. All our futures though have depended somehow on Charles.

I initially thought that this little Sarah was a, what you call - a nine day's wonder - a new flavour that would become more than ordinary. She was certainly not beautiful, and when her hair fell out and she shaved the rest, she looked like something one does not like to recall from the camps. I know some of us thought Rick and even Charles had gone mad. Only Dan loved her from the start. Charles had found her but she became Rick's new project: a new quest. He said it was important to, at least, try. And of course he has done what he wanted: to give her a new life.

I did think she might become a puppet only thinking what Rick did, but I remember one morning at breakfast, long past. He had said something to her when she looked around at him and said. "Do not presume to know what I am thinking, *all* of the time Richard." It hung in the air and he laughed. "Never Ms Townsend, never." We all relaxed.

I think it might be around this time that I realised she was the centre of my day. I would look forward to the sound of her talking to Beauty, to the ride, to her wave when she called, "See you tonight Patrice." To her staying to help with the horses: to her singing as she brushed. Orleans would snort almost in rhythm to her voice.

I remember the day she was singing in Welsh. I had asked her why she was learning Welsh and she laughed saying. "Oherwydd ei bod yn Patrice caled. It is difficult for me Patrice." And there she was: singing to Tinker – in Welsh – *The Salley Gardens*. So I joined in. In French of course. I can still hear that laugh as I sung. "Elle m'a demandé de prendre la vie facile. Comme l'herbe pousse sur les barrages; Mais j'étais jeune et stupide, et maintenant je suis plein de larmes." I thought it a special moment but she said. "It is a lament Patrice." I could see she understood me and that I would soon have to say Au Revoir to The Downs.

And so. Now I am here at *Les Arbres Bleus* with memories of Sally Townsend and my time at The Downs. I hear of course from Charles who tells me little. It is his way. I am to accompany him to Damascus in a week for a month with MSF. Rick and Bill follow later. Sally sends a postal every few months to let me know how the horses are and that Gregor is doing "a fine job." She tells me of other happenings and lately, that she is learning the Goldberg Variations. Nothing of what she thinks and feels. She always says she is missing me and I love her for it.

The Quarters

My first sighting of young Sally because I had been working up north, was to see her struggling to get down from one of the Prados telling Rick that she could manage. She stared at him until he stepped back and then she moved her legs around and slid from the seat. He opened the back door and handed her the crutches and off she went.

> Hi Bill. Sarah wants to look at the quarters. Would you show her around? I will only get in the way I'm sure. She wants to see where the teams sleep and everything. The men have left?

I thought then that Sally seemed to be more than just what we, or I, had thought. She certainly did want to see everything. She had never experienced living on a farm and so seeing the quarters was something new.

> These are dormitories! The men sleep together?

She had plenty of questions and I could see her making a mental note of everything I said and a visual note of what she saw as very basic living. It made me look at the rooms and what we provided although I have always thought our accommodation was the some of best I have seen.

> But Bill, it is so depressing. What do you think?

And it was what I think about Sally we all warmed to. We could see that she always wanted our side of everything to be considered and I had thought of perhaps suggesting we brighten the place up, have a separate kitchen, but ... Mind you there were times and situations where I have prayed to have somewhere like one of the dorms on which to lay my head, or be able to make a supper in the quarter's kitch.

But at that time, what could she do? Even if she wanted to. She was too ill, could hardly walk and I'm no doctor, but anyone could see she was getting worse. Greg and I came up to the house one evening and there was Sally whizzing around the lounge in a new electric wheelchair.

> *Look at this brand new toy Bill. Gregor look, it even lifts my legs for me. I can go up steps and lie back and look!*

With that she pressed the mobile and the seat lifted her high up, so that she was nearly able to talk face to face. She looked so happy, it was infectious. I saw Rick go to help Steph in the kitch and felt for him.

It was not long after this that Rick took her away. He said there was too much distraction at the The Downs and as winter was on the horizon, they would travel up north to warmer places. He was becoming haggard I think with worry. Not just for her but for us watching and wanting to care for her. I remember the day they left: Charles lifting her into her seat in the Winnebago which the boys had altered to a reclining position and was lined with pale blue sheepskin covers. The idea was to stay in resort hotels: the Bago was just "in case." They were towing our adapted Corolla and had all they needed for months on the road.

I wasn't the only one wondering if this was the last we would see of our Sally but as they wound their way down the hill with Patrice on Orleans to do gate opening, Charles said.

> *Don't concern yourselves lads. Her body may be weak, but her will is strong. Richard can work miracles.*

When was Charles not right? Ever since I met him first at Smyrna, he had that air of someone who almost knew how to hold the future and could plan what was best for all in the present. My first sight of him was through the smoke around us and the fire behind. He was not the captain of the boat we were struggling to reach, but he was there finding places for everyone they hauled from the sea.

When the boat turned and headed for Greece we were very low in the water. Gregorio had not fared well in the smoke and water and Rico (as Charles was then); found him a warm dry jacket. I can still see him with that haze and fire behind him telling my brother.

You will mend. Willhelm will see to it.

We saw him once again, at one end of a stretcher, when we landed, but it was not until we had arrived in France, that we again met Charles. He has been our brother ever since.

Of course when Sally returned with Rick she was a different Sally. We were expecting them but it was late in the day before they arrived. Dan had been down at the Gate House all day waiting. Stephane had held the evening meal and most of us were in the office with Charles trying not to watch the Gate House screen. And then they were there. We could see Dan rushing to open the gate waving, the Bago coming through and stopping, Dan beginning to rush to the passenger side, then changing and standing on the driver's runner.

Come on Daniele. Close the gate and get in.

It was Charles. We laughed because it was good to know Sally was driving. We could see them start off, then saw them reach the 5km marker. Stephane said,

I will bring soup in.

And so they arrived. We knew, of course, that Sally was much improved. Charles would never say much other than, *She's coming along.* And that was all. But the Sally who walked, yes walked, in with Dan almost pulling her, was a different girl. Yes, she looked well and could walk. Her smile though was brighter, not tinged with pain and her hair was now beautiful short brown curls.

She was hugging everyone, although she bowed to Charles which brought more laughter. There was much noise I remember. Gradually we moved to settle at the bench where Sally was pride of place. Rick was quiet. While Sally looked so healthy, he was sadly proud, looking on the verge of a sleep, which was why they had come home. It had taken almost a year to transform her, but I have always thought it perhaps took years from Rick's lifespan.

So our Sally just slipped back into life at The Downs and Rick recovered his spark. Sally though was definitely not the same. She wanted to fill every hour with work, study, music. She was engaged in all that went on at The Downs. So much energy it was infectious. It took time I think for her to begin to accept that there was a future: who would not? And so that is why we are now working on the new quarters. She gave me some plans about six months ago.

Quietly, quietly Bill. Just an idea.

And so, when she came down with Stephane, helping with the lunches and teas, we would just talk about the possibilities: whether this, whether that. And here we are, almost finished. Pool, Games Room, en-suites, the lot! The old quarters are to come down next week which is the biggest job because of the asbestos. Sally has made this a team effort – everyone's ideas – mine included. She calls it consensus and laughs.

This morning we were there looking at the paving around the pool when Charles arrived.

So Bill, almost done?
Sure is.
What do think about the paving Majesty? This from Sally.
Paving is paving Sarah.
But it could be at odd angles or boringly square on.
We have surgery in forty-five minutes.
I know, I know. Mr. Bennett needs a blood test, Mrs. Turner needs a repeat prescription. Oh and don't forget to take her B.P., and Mrs. O is Mrs. O, who just comes to see you. Their files are on the screen. I'll be there.
Good, good. See you Bill.

That was Charles. I saw him smile though as he turned his horse.

Paving!
He cares! You know he does. Maybe not about paving!

We laughed.

We both know his real cares, do we not? Leave it to you Bill?

I have always thought those two have something unusual that ties them together. Love? Never very sure about love.

The Opera

I had seen them before, he always immaculate in a tux which so few wear these days and his wife, always in sea colours, long, flowing. Of course, then, I did not know whether she was his wife. Just surmised you know. She was always different – just slightly. One would wonder, (well I did) what they did and if indeed they were married as they never stopped talking. They say the married ones never talk to one another, but then I am a romantic and I liked to think they were married and the exception. I may not be able to see you, but I know you are shrugging your shoulders darling.

Overhearing them once - it was always about what they were about to see - or at least I assumed, because I only heard them speaking once before in English. She seemed always to be the one who talked the most and he would listen, nod, shake his head or laugh. She had a way of counting off her points (assuming this was what she was doing) by placing her fingers one my one on the table as she talked and he would watch and his hands and his face would do the talking, either to agree or disagree. I remember feeling slightly annoyed, (well one would); when I had to break off to serve a customer.

Anyway, they would always come, usually on the second or third performance and she would find a place, he would sit and she would come up and order. Always with a "hallo again." She would ask my opinion of the opera or ballet and then say, "The truth?" And she would laugh, when I said, "Of course." But I never knew her name. She would always though thank me, saying, "I will remember our talk Louis." She was a doll. She knew the correct way to pronounce my name. Not the average punter.

And then there was the last time before I saw them again today. And it was really because of the new girl. The new girl was Ilse and I don't know how she became the new girl because her English was so poor.

If I had a dollar for every new girl! Well you know! Anyway they came in and could see there were no tables free so he sat on one of the counter stools whilst she placed her clutch bag on the one next and moved to order from the new girl. I was engrossed in taking orders for the interval drinks and when I looked up she gave me a little wave.

The new girl moved to serve her and took her order for the coffee which I helped dispense. She paid and moved to her stool. As I moved back and forth I caught pieces of their conversation. He was explaining, in English, how Aida is elevated because of her sacrifice. "Basura! It's just another, *'the girl has to die scenario'.*" And he laughed. I could see her looking at the tubs of cookies. I knew she would go for the macaroons.

When I next looked up she was ordering them, just two she said to the new girl. Ilse looked a little uncomfortable and moved to the wrong tub. And then I watched as she gave a slight wave and gently placed her hand on the correct jar's top, saying nothing but with a smile holding up two fingers. It was just like her. I noticed he was watching her too.

And then it all altered. She had turned her head slightly so that she could not help but see the background mirror which reflected the whole of the opera bar, including the counter. I saw her face change to panic and her hands reach out as her eyes closed. Then she fell.

He had seen it because he actually caught her before she hit the floor. When I reached them, her eyes opened. "Just a faint: just a faint Richard. I am fine." But, it was obvious he did not think it fine. "Would you call a taxi for us Louis? No, not an ambulance. A taxi."

And I did. There was one just dispensing a party. They were gone before the management even got to the bar. And that was that. I always wondered though what made her faint. Long time before I saw them again darling.

Until tonight. So, wait, and I'll tell you. They were not alone.

I know you do not like me talking of the past, but just, for a moment, listen.

Remember Beirut? Our escape and that ghastly awful night in the 70's when we thought it was the end? I know, wrong place, wrong time, but it wasn't was it? Remember the Czechs? Well, two of them were with my couple. Here for *Rigoletto*. And they remembered me.

Italy

We have only been in Florence three days, and I am sure she has spotted us already but I must be anxious to follow Charles' directions and just "stay on track" which is his way of saying: follow the instructions. Can you believe this! Never visited with Florence before? Surely a sin for all for Italians. To be fair, it would have changed much although those old buildings, ah me!

It is as though we have been given a tour because the lovely one surely would have visited the Uffizi before we arrived. But in the last days we have seen the Corridoio Vasariano, the Palazzo del Bargello, and the wonderful Cattedrale di Santa Maria del Flore, the boy giving me the history of each. Already I know this.

And I am sure she knows when these feet are wearying and I needed to sit. She just stops, looks round, and Bravo - heads towards the nearest ristorante - where we can hide ourselves and rest from the heat.

And then today the sweet lovely lady did what all the lovely ladies I have consorted with through my very long life did: she changes her mind.

The boy was talking about gelato when the Cameriere leaned over me. "Signore, Scusa. The young lady wishes for you to join her." He pointed, and there was the lovely, waving and laughing her laugh.

We, as any gentlemen would, did not waste time. The boy saying his usual, what fun, what fun! The lovely saying it was time to join up was it not? Where would I like to go, she, knowing my desire to visit, some day, the old Italy? We could go anywhere! And the boy saying Charles will not be content. The lovely saying Charles need never know – a white lie – yes! Me, I love white lies. Good not to tell to Charles: only a little, sometimes. And I know he will laugh and perhaps have planned this.

So you see this is why we now head south to our old home and where the boy was born so long ago now, I almost forget. To the Florence of the south and I am wishing so much that alterations will be not so much that I cannot remember the alleys of my youth. It was done. The lovely one arranged for the vehicle and we were off from our hotel in the noon of the day.

So wonderful. I am hoping so much that home villa will be there. The place where the boy was born. Where my mother and father raised me. It is not good to go back they say, but our hearts do not obey rules. Is it not so?

***

And so, we came to Lecce, where we spent just the afternoon. And then onto Vernole which in my day was just a few families living. The lovely one said we should stay somewhere "with five stars" and so we are resident in the Relais Masseria Le Cesine. The boy is already soaking himself in the pool. I do not recognize anything of the village I once knew. We shall see.

The lovely one has taken a taxi to the Bibioteca Comunale to see if she can locate my old home. She is sure she can find some old maps which will have the village laid out. Now we are here I know I cannot find the past. It is however, not forgotten. But there is much of Italy I would erase from my past.

The boy waves and I know he likes me see how well he does in the water. He is swimming lengths. Always slowly but well. His blue maglietta covers most of him. He says he is beating his record. I am full of the pride and love.

I remember when the lovely one first saw him without his clothes. It was in one of his sleeping times and we had decided to shower him to cool, when suddenly she was there, looking at my poor boy's body. He was lying on his front and she could see all the damage that his spine and legs had suffered. Her look was not of horror but of sad understanding. All she said was, *Josiah*.

What can one say to those who have not experienced the hatred people have for Jews or anyone they feel is inferior. She knew of course how it can rob families of loved ones and of our history. Of what has been done and is still done to Jews throughout the world. It seems humans will always breed hatred for those who are different.

The powerlessness I remember the most. I try to forget when they hauled my boy from us. He would not be quiet yelling at those who had gathered to just look at our sorry group who were waiting for transport to Tiburtina station.

He kept his litany up: *Sono italiano, Noi siamo* until they took him from us. And there in the piazza, they tied him to a pilastro and from the soldiers came one waving a whip. I cannot forget the sound it made. From the beginning my son did not scream or cry. For a while he kept up his *Sono italiano* and then became silent. My neighbour said, *Do not look Josiah.* But I did. I would not look away. I saw his back begin to bleed, his legs break. I saw him lose consciousness.

Then there was the bus and our future changed. From it stepped a German Army Officer and the whipping soldier stopped for one moment before he crumbled to the asphalt. The Officer said nothing and turned to look at those guarding us. Then, behold, they put down their rifles and lay face down on the ground.

Please to board the bus he said to us, speaking the Italian. And so we did. There was another officer helping us into the bus who looked at me. "Do not concern, we will bring your son." And they did. There was a stretcher born by the officers and the bus was away.

The journey was not a long one. It was one of many stops to freedom. We were hastened into a Catholic Church some way from Rome where we were welcomed, ah, I remember, so well. The next time I saw the officers, they were officers no more. That was when I met our brothers, Charles and Richard as they now are. They who saved the life of my boy and many others.

106

So you see. All the lovely one saw were the scars which remain on the boy's body. The poor body which my saviours could not heal back to perfection, who did what they always will: their best. She did not want explanations but her tears were enough. Then she gently placed her hand on the scars and leaned over and kissed them.

The boy, of course, does not know this. Apart from me, only Charles was there. Now, only a few of us have seen his scars. The shuffling walk is there for all to see and is much like the palsy. And now we have good lives in Australia with no fear of those jackboots.

And here in Vernole, the lovely one has returned with much information and copies of long ago maps of the village. So we plan to go in search of my old home. An adventure she calls it. The boy is also eager to see where he was born although he remembers little of the time Lia and I were there.

***

And so the next morning we will go in search of Via IV Novembre and, of course, we will find it. We will leave the auto to walk. Nothing will look as I remembered but I will see where there is another road: the corner houses might be the same. And then it will be easy, when we reach the corner. I will see the old church tower in the distance. Then we will just turn and see that the villa which stood where I had once lived is no longer there. True there will be a villa, but nothing like the plain adobe I remember. True it will have a flat roof where they sleep in the heat as we used to but no, it will not be my old place. I will say to the lovely one my thanks and the boy will be sad. And we will return to our five star and plan where to visit with next.

The Wedding

Why she wanted to spend so much time in Italy is beyond me. But then much about Sarah still has the power to perplex me. She wants to "come down to earth!" To be "in control!" And, of course I know what she means. So, here we are. None of us minded going back to anywhere in Europe, but *Italy! It's the Renaissance, Charles.* As if I did not know and that other countries were subsumed by it: had their cultures altered for ever. Give me the Dutch every time.

I digress. It has come down to me being here because everyone has done more than their share of this *Sarah Project* and as it was reaching the deadline of her "six months," I thought now she seemed to have made Rome her last (and I sincerely hope it is the last) place to visit, I would play bodyguard. I must admit she has travelled far. I envied Bill joining her on the Canadian rail crossing; and Patrice, from Paris to St. Petersburg and The Hermitage. Perhaps next year.

So here I am, in a café called *Cantina Maria,* where Sarah has come for breakfast for the last couple of weeks. They do serve good coffee and croissants, which is what we are both eating at present, although not together. I am wearing dark glasses, a flowered shirt (I shudder), chinos and, an English Heritage baseball cap! Stephane would say, "Idi lik."

I have two newspapers, *la Repubblica* (interesting) and *il Tempo* (more than interesting) which I am skirting through at present but will attend to more thoroughly this evening. It is illuminating to see this country not altering their adherence to borderline fascism and a tendency to circumnavigate laws. I am reading about the refugee situation in Sicily which is becoming acute. They feel left in the lurch by the EU. They – both the refugees and the citizens are becoming restless – feeling nothing is being done to solve problems which are arising. Lack of money, no planning and no accommodation. I wonder how history will remember Chancellor Merkel.

I keep one eye on *The Proje*ct who is, of course, reading. I watched her the other day sitting on a wall by the fountain in front of the

Medici Villa in the shaded sun, not noticing that a breeze had sprung up and was gently causing the water to spray her back. Or, perhaps, she did know and liked it. I think she knew.

She is sitting, not actually with her back to me, but side on and I have a good view of all the café. The morning is pleasant, not too hot. I am hoping that *The Project* will decide to have a day where I can easily follow her: not too much walking in the sun. I relax into my reading of the headlines looking up occasionally and I have actually had to raise my newspaper higher because Richard, yes it is Richard, has just walked in. He is supposed to be holding the fort at The Downs!

He cannot have seen her, because he has walked to the counter and spoken to the Cameriere, who has pointed to a table for two by the door which is vacant and given him a menu.

He turns, and that is when he sees her. It is obvious that he did not know she was here and turns to look around, I think to find me. My disguise must work, plus the slouching body language I have practised because he begins to look outside, wondering where I must be. And then she looks up and sees him. His arms go out and he shrugs. She is up, but they do not hug, just touch hands. They are both talking, I think in Italian. Crazy!

So, I am watching them both! Should I retire? End *The Project*? Did she know? *What,* is he doing here?

They are just sitting opposite one another. His coffee arrives and I escape. I wander casually (I hope) over to the chess tables outside the café's competitor and join a group of elderly men engrossed in the game. What I really would like to do is shake him and find out who has taken up the reins at home. It must be Stephane.

And here I am, watching a game of chess in Rome! And if that gentleman does not move his Queen's Bishop, he has had it. I am thinking that I must away to my *lo albergo* and begone. And then the two leave the Cantina Maria. She takes his arm and I know from the small smile that he is where we would all like to be. And so I just follow...

I am developing a limp to go with my walking stick and hope I look as though I am in my eighth decade with a needed hip-replacement. I remember when acting that the hardest thing for a young actor was to take on the role of someone aged and infirm. The best I ever saw was Patrick Stewart, but then Stewart was old at twenty. Russell Beale does a splendid Lear, but then he is getting on. So I am trying for a Stewart/Beale old man.

They are heading for the, where are we now? North of the Vatican and just passing the Roma Balduina. Ah, heading for the park. I sit on a plinth surrounding a none-too-prepossessing sculpture of a female: nude of course. They have forked right and have stopped in the middle of the pathway. There is something wrong. Richard has his arms wide. Must I hear this? And yes.

She says, "Of course." And she puts her arms around him and he encloses her. Then she holds his hand and leads him to a seat. He does not look happy though and they sit and she begins to talk, not looking at him but at his hand which she still holds. She is telling him about the night they went to see Aida (when was that?). He interrupts her (for Darwin's sake Richard!), but she holds up her other hand to stop him, shaking her head.

And so Sarah tells him what I have known for at least two years and my dearest friend has not seen. She stops talking, then raises his hand and kisses it.

It is the sweetest moment and I look away. What a time it has taken. I would be the first to admit when I met Sarah that it was a risk. They have both proved me wrong in so many ways. I do not look again and start walking.

I muse that I may be able to get a flight out of Rome this afternoon or evening which would make me well on the way home by tomorrow. I am wondering what those two will do now. I am leaving the park when I hear someone running behind me. I have forgotten the limp and have been spotted.

> *No Hallo, Buddy?* I turn.
> *You have not called me that in a while.*

Sarah is at his side. Both look: what is that cloud number when people are over the moon? It warmed my heart.

> *You spotted me?*
> *With the chess players. Charles, you cannot fail to be recognised. Italians are not a tall race, generally. You just stand out! Six foot four and limping!*
> *So disguise a failure. Did you spot me Sarah?*
> *No, I thought – at last – I was alone.*

She thinks she has perfected fooling me.

> *My apologies, but – hey – it was not my idea. We just wanted to make sure…*
> *I know. I know, she says.*

It's the nose, the eyes and of course, the smile.

> *Do you think you can work your magic? We want to be really married. A wedding. Here: just a simple one.*
> *A wedding!*

***

Nothing is ever simple for these two! The conclusion to my magic, of course, happened today. One would be forgiven for believing that the only places of worship in Rome would be Roman Catholic. Not so. I found a delightful Baptist Church with a most obliging Pastor and it was easier than I thought to obtain both the *Atto Notorio* from the Tribunale Civile de Roma and the *Nulla Osta* from the Australian Embassy. Money always helps: especially in Italy.

So here we all are.   Patrice arrived a couple of hours ago from Provence. He has Sarah on his arm and is walking her into the church while we wait with the Pastor. There are quite a few people here, the Pastor's wife having produced "guests." We three, Richard, Patrice and I have managed to find grey Edwardian suits with blue ties and waistcoats. Grey toppers of course. Richard is the happiest I have seen him in years. And Sarah is a dream in a blue gossamer dress with daisies and blue ribbons, I think, in her hair.

The service is simple, brief and in English. They exchange different rings from those they already wore. I wonder what the Pastor and his congregation would think if they knew our beliefs and whether they would accept our respect for history and its gifts, but not the foundation on which religion flourishes.

Sarah's camera takes our likeness for the albums: Patrice not allowed to use his Smartphone. He smiles and says, "You cannot fight it, Mon frère." We adjourn to the hall where the Pastor has allowed me to arrange a small repast. I watch Sarah gently including everyone, making sure each is thanked for attending this special day. The Pastor and his wife are delighted at an enjoyable unexpected event for the church.

There is one, who though present at the ceremony, does not attend this part of the celebration. In the church he had remained at the rear, standing, regal as ever. We had met at first light where he came, not from his homeland Brittany, but from lovely Devon. It is years since we have met. He looked, as always, the aesthete, but who could, on the turn, become a monk, a beggar or a company director. There was so little time to convey our news, our plans and aspirations, but he was here for her and to see her become one with Richard whom he loves as a son. I treasure the short time I had with him.

Patrice strolls (he never walks, just strolls or runs) towards me.

So, Charles, we lose.

I do not rise to the bait.

Be rational as you would say. One is never rational in love, n'est-ce pas? Patrice: far too passionate, far too romantic. Vous, far too rational. Young Rick's love, of course, is a disease and would slowly eat him away. The lovely Sally has saved him. Hers is a devotional love. They have saved one another. I could quite easily run him through! You laugh. Being rational though, one still would not get the lady. I wish he was not so bloody good and had not saved my life: more than once. You saw Edwyn? Ah, of course you did. You have a room booked for me?

I laugh and say yes, in a cheap pension where we are now all staying. *Merde* he cries. I trust no-one has heard. I look forward to our evening meal. It will be like having him home again. I miss him, though it is good to have him in France.

And it was. The three of us and Sarah: all in tune. I looked at her throughout the evening and wondered if she knew. And now, we are about to depart. Richard and Sarah off to Anglesey. I sputtered but Sarah explained she wants to walk the Menai Straits. Homage *"to the best engineers the world has known."* Then to Southampton, and the QE2 to New York. Across the States by rail. To Sydney and home. The end of *The Sarah Project:* or this *Sarah Project*.

Me, I am to accompany Patrice to his palatial residence where he wishes me to admire what he has done to restore ceilings and to meet his Maria. Bill and Gregor say everything is fine back home. Harvesting is a way off. So, back to Provence with Patrice for a visit. It will be good to see it again.

A Concert

It is concert day. That is what Clive has been calling it these past weeks. There are many of our friends here and it is a happy atmosphere. The children have been enjoying the pool for hours, even though it is autumn. Parents have taken the little ones in as well. Sarah went in with our little Daisy. She is about to have our third child. Charles was also in the pool, our son Danny on his back. Stacey and her friends practised backward flips to great acclaim.

Stephane thinks he has everything organised. And it is. There is always an atmosphere here that can be seen in few gatherings. Not that I attend many other gatherings. Sometimes though, it is necessary. Here the only stimulants are the company and eyes are bright. All the lads in the team are here with their wives and children. So many children!

Everyone seems to be talking, but there is no noise. I love the sounds of so much talk, but so little noise. There is the sound of ping pong balls with hurrahs from table tennis. Gregor is juggling with some of the children. Others play Monopoly. Clive is playing chess with Daniele: trying still to beat him. There is music coming from the main house. Most of the men are playing Boules on the lawn. From the laughter, it is clear that Patrice's team is winning.

Most of the activity is happening in what we like to call *l'addition*. I love the house though and I am glad we brought it here although everyone thought I was mad. The house is of that period in Australian architecture priding itself in upholding tradition, insisting on all-round verandahs, high ceilings and large rooms. We have kept to this tradition, the rooms being furnished from a century past. There are paintings everywhere, some very old, others contemporary. Bill is really good, especially with oils and there is one of his in the kitchen: very abstract. I like the ceramics Stephane has made which use Victorian motifs. A prized possession though is one of Morgona's paintings which used to hang at our house in Applethwaite. It is of the valley seen from the top field.

We have eaten early: a splendid affair. We had more long tables with everyone on benches. Children are always included with the adults here at meal times. Stephane usually has the pans on the side and everyone helps themselves, but today bowls and platters were on the tables, everyone helping each other.

I like to watch the interactions committing them to my mind's eye photographic album. Nancy spent much time talking to Maria who was sitting opposite. Maria would be one of the most beautiful women to grace these tables. Very French of course. She had her little girl next to her and every now and then would say, "en anglais s'il vous plaît Catherine," which made the child giggle. Maria seems to fit in well here and Sarah and she have become firm friends.

As the light begins to fade, we have arranged the seats to face the baby grand which has been moved from the house to l'addition. Gregor is handing out cushions and blankets to stave off the evening air because the doors are all open. The youngsters are arranging themselves on the floor in the front for a good view. Daniele is there showing them how to pluck a violin and tap on its belly. When Bill comes in carrying his bass, he has to follow suit. I love the way Daniele is with children. One could easily say that he is a child himself but it is not that. It is his unimaginable love for everyone he meets.

I see Clive has moved to sit with his mother and father. They are justly proud of him. He is soon to fly to America and start university at Princeton where he has been given a scholarship. I am also proud of this young man who has really done this on his own with little help from me. He will do well there and love it. I still have friends there who will be his guides and mentors.

Our concert begins. Groups have been running off to rehearsals since morning and there is a growing air of excitement. Nancy has helped the girls with their song and thinks it will be lovely. They are going to sing a song from *Frozen* which they have all seen and fallen in love with. I am supposed to know the play list, but there is always much that is unexpected at our concerts.

Quietly, Gregor sits down at the piano and begins to play. It is something Scottish. The girls sitting in the front get up and begin to twirl around a la *Frozen*. Bill has joined him quietly on bass. Gregor finishes with a flourish which the girls love. I am signed to join the others and violins and violas are appearing from everywhere. Sarah is there with my cello. She gives our daughter Daisy to Stephane who is sitting in the front with little Danny and Goldie at his feet. Bill gives his bass another spin which delights everyone and then begins a beat. One by one we join him. There is Charles, Josh and Daniele, plus Patrice and Sarah all playing violins or violas. Gradually we cruise into the Beatles' *Penny Lane*.

When we finish there is a pause. Daniele places his violin on his chair and is joined by Bill and Eddie's sons, Sean and Clive. Charles and I begin to play and the three boys start singing the Beatles' *Blackbird*. Their voices harmonise and blend with us. It is well done if a little over the heads of the children.

Then it is the turn of the girls with their Anna song from *Frozen*, *For the First Time in Forever*. There are six of them, all ages. Even Patrice and Maria's Catherine is there doing all the moves and signs, Gregor at the piano leading.

There is much fuss next as it is the men's turn. Some of us are trying to remember where we should stand. The string players, plus Gregor and Bill are all there with the other men and boys. I have been looking forward to this and hoping I remember what to do.

It is just a hum at first then the boys start a beat with their hands, a slow clap. Then Sean begins singing as we all slap our thighs in unison. It is from *Seven Brides for Seven Brothers: the Polecat Song*. We are all swaying, slapping and clapping, keeping in time wonderfully. There is great stomping at the finish and much laughter.

Clive who has been helping everyone organise rehearsals for this evening has helped the women decide also on the *Seven Brides* because they now follow with *June Bride* although clearly there are three of them in various stages of pregnancy. With the mixture of voices though, they do sound bridal: very 1950s.

The next piece is so different. When everyone is quiet, Gregor produces what he calls a flute but his flute is different. It is coloured and when he begins to play Bill starts singing. This would stop anyone in their tracks because the sound is from the past. It is a chant: an Armenian Sharakan hymn I remember from long ago. The sound is stringently sad but this does not stop two small girls from dancing to it with ballet steps.

And then it is all the musicians back together to play *Fiddlers' Sundays* which gathers momentum until everyone is clapping and thinking they could not go faster. The audience is delighted by the trios and duos, all trying to outdo one another. Charles, Patrice and Daniele make for great laughter as they try to beat one another.

When the clapping finishes, it is my turn introduce our last piece, but I hesitate. So my lovely Sarah moves to Stephane, takes our daughter from him and hands her to me. Little Danny runs to sit on Charles' lap. Sarah then turns and moves to the piano and adjusts the stool to some smiles. Goldie settles herself at Sarah's feet.

It is late piano piece by Brahms, whose birthday anniversary it is today but only a few know this. One can see, however, the *"Maestro's"* birthday is important because Stephane is clearly affected. It is an *Intermezzo* in a minor key. Stephane sits and quietly moves his head and begins weeping. Charles has also covered his face in the hair of my son. To mitigate a picture that threatens sadness, those small girls in the front again stand and begin to dance to Sarah's playing. It completes the picture. When the last notes are played and the applause is heard, Stephane goes to her and as she turns he covers her face with kisses.

This piece finishes our May concert. There is hot cocoa and buns and much laughter and reminiscing before adults and children depart to the various places of rest. Daisy sleeps in my arms and I see Danny is about to follow his sister as he settles in Charles' arms. I marvel at how good he is with not only our children, but all the children we have known throughout our lives.

The autumn night air is cold, filled with stars. It holds the music with the Brahms refusing to leave.

Frances Richardson lives in Perth, Western Australia. She has a degree in Literature and Creative Writing from Curtin University, winning the inaugural prize for Creative Writing. She has been anthologised and won prizes for both her short fiction and poetry. Other interests, when not writing, are the theatre, philosophy, freedom and its constraints, all forms of art, space (wants to see the James Webb launched), science, time, baroque music, actor Richard Armitage, and Star Trek.

Other works by Frances Richardson:

Rear View Images - Poetry

Cafe Love and other Writings - Short Fiction/Essays:

millrun – An Anthology of Writing/Art/Photography